Anything Is Possible

Anything Is Possible

ELIZABETH STROUT

RANDOM HOUSE

NEW YORK

Copyright © 2017 by Elizabeth Strout

Published in the United States by Random House, an imprint and division of Penguin Random House LLC, New York.

RANDOM HOUSE and the HOUSE colophon are registered trademarks of Penguin Random House LLC.

"Snow-Blind" was published, in slightly different form, in the Spring 2013 issue of *Virginia Quarterly Review.*

LIBRARY OF CONGRESS CATALOGING-IN-PUBLICATION DATA
Names: Strout, Elizabeth, author.
Title: Anything is possible : fiction / Elizabeth Strout.
Description: New York : Random House, [2017]
Identifiers: LCCN 2016020620 | ISBN 9780812989403 |
ISBN 9780812989427 (ebook)
Subjects: LCSH: Mothers and daughters—Fiction. | Brothers and sisters—Fiction. | Families—Fiction. | Domestic fiction.
Classification: LCC PS3569.T736 A6 2017 | DDC 813/.54—dc23
LC record available at https://lccn.loc.gov/2016020620

Printed in the United States of America on acid-free paper

randomhousebooks.com

2 4 6 8 9 7 5 3 1

FIRST EDITION

Book design by Dana Leigh Blanchette

For my brother,
Jon Strout

CONTENTS

Anything Is Possible

The Sign

Tommy Guptill had once owned a dairy farm, which he'd inherited from his father, and which was about two miles from the town of Amgash, Illinois. This was many years ago now, but at night Tommy still sometimes woke with the fear he had felt the night his dairy farm burned to the ground. The house had burned to the ground as well; the wind had sent sparks onto the house, which was not far from the barns. It had been his fault—he always thought it was his fault—because he had not checked that night on the milking machines to make sure they had been turned off properly, and this is where the fire started. Once it started, it ripped with a fury over the whole place. They lost everything, except for the brass frame to the living room mirror, which he came upon in the rubble the next day, and he left it where it was. A collection was taken up: For a number of weeks his kids went to school in the clothes of their classmates, until he could gather himself and the little money he had; he sold the land to the neighboring farmer, but it did not bring much money in. Then he and his wife, a short pretty woman named Shirley, bought new clothes, and he bought a house as well, Shirley keeping her spirits up admirably as all this was going on. They'd had to buy a house in Amgash, which was a run-down town, and his kids went to school there instead of in Carlisle, where they had been able to go to school before, his farm being just on the line dividing the two towns. Tommy took a job as the janitor in the Amgash school system; the steadiness of the job appealed to him, and he could never go to work on someone else's farm, he did not have the stomach for that. He was thirty-five years old at the time.

The kids were grown now, with kids of their own who were also grown, and he and Shirley still lived in their small house; she had planted flowers around it, which was unusual in that town. Tommy had worried a good deal about his children at the time of the fire; they had gone from having their home be a place that class trips came to—each year in spring the fifth-grade class from Carlisle would make a day of it, eating their lunches out beside the barns on the wooden tables there, then tromping through the barns watching the men milking the cows, the white foamy stuff going up and over them in the clear plastic pipes—to having to see their father as the man who pushed the broom over the "magic dust" that got tossed over the throw-up of some kid who had been sick in the hallways, Tommy wearing his gray pants and a white shirt that had *Tommy* stitched on it in red.

Well. They had all lived through it.

＊

This morning Tommy drove slowly to the town of Carlisle for errands; it was a sunny Saturday in May, and his wife's eighty-second birthday was just a few days away. All around him were open fields, the corn newly planted, and the soybeans too. A number of fields were still brown, as they'd been plowed under for their planting, but mostly there was the high blue sky, with a few white clouds scattered near the horizon. He drove past the sign on the road that led down to the Barton home; it still said SEWING AND ALTERATIONS, even though the woman, Lydia Barton, who did the sewing and alterations had died many years ago. The Barton family had been outcasts, even in a town like Amgash, their extreme poverty and strangeness making this so. The oldest child, a man named Pete, lived alone there now, the middle child was two towns away, and the youngest, Lucy Barton, had fled many years ago, and had ended up living in New York City. Tommy had spent time thinking of Lucy. All those years she had lingered after school, alone in a classroom, from fourth grade right up to her senior year in high school; it had taken her a few years to even look him in the eye.

But now Tommy was driving past the area where his

farm had been—these days it was all fields, not a sign of the
farm was left—and he thought, as he often thought, about
his life back then. It had been a good life, but he did not
regret the things that had happened. It was not Tommy's
nature to regret things, and on the night of the fire—in the
midst of his galloping fear—he understood that all that
mattered in this world were his wife and his children, and
he thought that people lived their whole lives not knowing
this as sharply and constantly as he did. Privately, he
thought of the fire as a sign from God to keep this gift
tightly to him. Privately, because he did not want to be
thought of as a man who made up excuses for a tragedy;
and he did not want anyone—not even his dearly beloved
wife—to think he would do this. But he had felt that night,
while his wife kept the children over by the road—he had
rushed them from the house when he saw that the barn was
on fire—as he watched the enormous flames flying into the
nighttime sky, then heard the terrible screaming sounds of
the cows as they died, he had felt many things, but it was
just as the roof of his house crashed in, fell into the house
itself, right into their bedrooms and the living room below
with all the photos of the children and his parents, as he
saw this happen he had felt—undeniably—what he could
only think was the presence of God, and he understood
why angels had always been portrayed as having wings, because there had been a sensation of that—of a rushing
sound, or not even a sound, and then it was as though God,
who had no face, but was God, pressed up against him and

conveyed to him without words—so briefly, so fleetingly—
some message that Tommy understood to be: *It's all right,
Tommy.* And then Tommy had understood that it was all
right. It was beyond his understanding, but it was all right.
And it had been. He often thought that his children had
become more compassionate as a result of having to go to
school with kids who were poor, and not from homes like
the one they had first known. He had felt the presence of
God since, at times, as though a golden color was very near
to him, but he never again felt visited by God as he had felt
that night, and he knew too well what people would make
of it, and this is why he would keep it to himself until his
dying day—the sign from God.

Still, on a spring morning as this one was, the smell of
the soil brought back to him the smells of the cows, the
moisture of their nostrils, the warmth of their bellies, and
his barns—he had had two barns—and he let his mind roll
over pieces of scenes that came to him. Perhaps because he
had just passed the Barton place he thought of the man,
Ken Barton, who had been the father of those poor, sad
children, and who had worked on and off for Tommy, and
then he thought—as he more often did—of Lucy, who had
left for college and then ended up in New York City. She
had become a writer.

Lucy Barton.

Driving, Tommy shook his head slightly. Tommy knew
many things as a result of being the janitor in that school
more than thirty years; he knew of girls' pregnancies and

drunken mothers and cheating spouses, for he overheard
these things talked about by the students in their small hud-
dles by the bathrooms, or near the cafeteria; in many ways
he was invisible, he understood that. But Lucy Barton had
troubled him the most. She and her sister, Vicky, and her
brother, Pete, had been viciously scorned by the other kids,
and by some of the teachers too. Yet because Lucy stayed
after school so often for so many years he felt—though she
seldom spoke—that he knew her the best. One time when
she was in the fourth grade, it was his first year working
there, he had opened the door to a classroom and found her
lying on three chairs pushed together, over near the radiators, her coat as a blanket, fast asleep. He had stared at her,
watching her chest move slightly up and down, seen the
dark circles beneath her eyes, her eyelashes spread like tiny
twinkling stars, for her eyelids had been moist as though
she had been weeping before she slept, and then he backed
out slowly, quietly as he could; it had felt almost unseemly
to come upon her like that.

But one time—he remembered this now—she must have
been in junior high school, and he'd walked into the classroom and she was drawing on the blackboard with chalk.
She stopped as soon as he stepped inside the room. "You go
ahead," he said. On the board was a drawing of a vine with
many small leaves. Lucy moved away from the blackboard,
then she suddenly spoke to him. "I broke the chalk," she
said. Tommy told her that was fine. "I did it on purpose,"
she said, and there was a tiny glint of a smile before she

looked away. "On purpose?" he asked, and she nodded, again with the tiny smile. So he went and picked up a piece of chalk, a full stick of it, and he snapped it in half and winked at her. In his memory she had *almost* giggled. "You drew that?" he asked, pointing to the vine with the small leaves. And she shrugged then and turned away. But usually, she was just sitting at a desk and reading, or doing her homework, he could see that she was doing that.

He pulled up to a stop sign now, and said the words aloud to himself quietly, "Lucy, Lucy, Lucy B. Where did you go to, how did you flee?"

He knew how. In the spring of her senior year, he had seen her in the hallway after school, and she had said to him, so suddenly open-faced, her eyes big, "Mr. Guptill, I'm going to college!" And he had said, "Oh, Lucy. That's wonderful." She had thrown her arms around him; she would not let go, and so he hugged her back. He always remembered that hug, because she had been so thin; he could feel her bones and her small breasts, and because he wondered later how much—how little—that girl had ever been hugged.

Tommy pulled away from the stop sign and drove into the town; right there beyond was a parking space. Tommy pulled in to it, got out of his car, and squinted in the sunshine. "Tommy Guptill," shouted a man, and, turning, Tommy saw Griff Johnson walking toward him with his characteristic limp, for Griff had one leg that was shorter than the other, and even his built-up shoe could not keep him from limping. Griff had an arm out, ready to shake hands. "Griffith," said Tommy, and they pumped their arms for a long time, while cars drove slowly past them down Main Street. Griff was the insurance man here in town, and he had been awfully good to Tommy; learning that Tommy had not insured his farm for its worth, Griff had said, "I met you too late," which was true. But Griff, with his warm face, and big belly now, continued to be good to Tommy. In fact, Tommy did not know anyone—he thought—who was not good to him. As a breeze moved around them, they spoke of their children and grandchildren; Griff had a grandson who was on drugs, which Tommy thought was very sad, and he just listened and nodded, glancing up at the trees that lined Main Street, their leaves so young and bright green, and then he listened about another grandson who was in medical school now, and Tommy said, "Hey, that's just great, good for him," and they clapped hands on each other's shoulders and moved on.

In the dress shop, with its bell that announced his entrance, was Marilyn Macauley, trying on a dress. "Tommy, what brings you in here?" Marilyn was thinking of getting the dress for her granddaughter's baptism a few Sundays from now, she said, and she tugged on the side of it; it was beige with swirling red roses; she was without her shoes, standing in just her stockings. She said that it was an extravagance to buy a new dress for such a thing, but that she felt like it. Tommy—who had known Marilyn for years, first when she was in high school as a student in Amgash—

saw her embarrassment, and he said he didn't think it was
an extravagance at all. Then he said, "When you have a
chance, Marilyn, can you help me find something for my
wife?" He saw her become efficient then, and she said yes,
she certainly would, and she went into the changing room
and came back out in her regular clothes, a black skirt and
a blue sweater, with her flat black shoes on, and right away
she took Tommy over to the scarves. "Here," she said, pulling out a red scarf that had a design with gold threads running through it. Tommy held it, but picked up a flowery
scarf with his other hand. "Maybe this," he said. And Marilyn said, "Yes, that looks like Shirley," and then Tommy
understood that Marilyn liked the red scarf herself but
would never allow herself to buy it. Marilyn, that first year
Tommy worked as a janitor, had been a lovely girl, saying
"Hi, Mr. Guptill!" whenever she saw him, and now she had
become an older woman, nervous, thin, her face pinched.
Tommy thought what other people thought, it was because
her husband had been in Vietnam and had never afterward
been the same; Tommy would see Charlie Macauley around
town, and he always looked so far away, the poor man, and
poor Marilyn too. So Tommy held the red scarf with the
gold threads for a minute as though considering it, then
said, "I think you're right, this one looks more like Shirley,"
and took the flowery one to the register. He thanked Marilyn for her help.

"I think she'll love it," Marilyn said, and Tommy said he
was sure she would.

Back on the sidewalk, Tommy walked up to the bookstore. He thought there might be a gardening book his wife would like; once he was inside he walked about, then saw—right there in the middle of the store—a display of a new Lucy Barton book. He picked it up—it had on its cover a city building—then he looked at the back flap, where her picture was. He thought he wouldn't recognize her if he met her now, it was only because he knew it was her that he could see the remnants of her, in her smile, still a shy smile. He was reminded once again of the afternoon she said she had broken the chalk on purpose, her funny little smile that day. She was an older woman now, and the photo showed her hair pulled back, and the more he looked at it, the more he could see the girl she had been. Tommy moved out of the way of a mother with two small children, she moved past him with the kids and said, "'Scuse me, sorry," and he said, "Oh sure," and then he wondered—as he sometimes did—what Lucy's life had been like, so far away in the City of New York.

He put the book back on the display and went to find the salesclerk to ask about a book on gardening. "I might have just the thing, we *just* got this in," and the girl—who was not a girl, really, except they all seemed like girls to Tommy these days—brought him a book with hyacinths on the cover, and he said, "Oh, that's perfect." The girl asked if he wanted it wrapped, and he said Yes, that would be great, and he watched while she spread the silver paper around it, with her fingernails that were painted blue, and with her

tongue sticking slightly out, between her teeth, as she con-
centrated; she put the Scotch tape on, then gave him a big
smile when it was done. "That's perfect," he repeated, and
she said, "You have a nice day now," and he told her the
same. He left the store and walked across the street in the
bright sunshine; he would tell Shirley about Lucy's book;
she had loved Lucy because he had. Then he started the car
and pulled out of the parking space, started back down the
road toward home.

The Johnson boy came to Tommy's mind, how he
couldn't get off drugs, and then Tommy thought of Marilyn Macauley and her husband, Charlie, and then his mind
went to his older brother, who had died a few years back,
and he thought how his brother—who had been in World
War II, who had been at the camps when they were being
emptied—he thought how his brother had returned from
the war a different man; his marriage ended, his children
disliked him. Not long before his brother died, he told
Tommy about what he had seen in the camps, and how he
and the others had the job of taking the townspeople
through them. They had somehow taken a group of women
from the town through the camps to show them what had
been right there, and Tommy's brother said that although
some of the women wept, some of them put their chins up,
and looked angry, as if they refused to be made to feel bad.
This image had always stayed with Tommy, and he wondered why it came to him now. He unrolled the window all
the way down. It seemed the older he grew—and he had

grown old—the more he understood that he could not understand this confusing contest between good and evil, and
that maybe people were not meant to understand things
here on earth.

But as he approached the sign that declared SEWING
AND ALTERATIONS, he slowed his car and turned down
the long road that led to the Barton house. Tommy had
made a practice of checking in on Pete Barton, who of
course was not a kid now but an older man, ever since
Ken—Pete's father—had died. Pete had stayed living in the
house alone, and Tommy had not seen him for a couple of
months.

Down the long road he drove, it was isolated out here, a
thing he and Shirley had discussed over the years, isolation
not being a good thing for the kids. There were cornfields
on one side and soybean fields on the other. The single
tree—huge—that had been in the middle of the cornfields
had been struck by lightning a few years back, and it lay
now on its side, the long branches bare and broken and
poking up toward the sky.

The truck was there next to the small house, which had
not been painted in so many years it looked washed out, the
shingles pale, some missing. The blinds were drawn, as they
always were, and Tommy got out of his car and went and
knocked on the door. Standing in the sunshine, he thought
again of Lucy Barton, how she had been a skinny child,
painfully so, and her hair was long and blond, and almost
never did she look him in the eye. Once, when she was still

so young, he had walked into a classroom after school and found her sitting there reading, and she had jumped—he saw her really jump with fear—when the door opened. He had said to her quickly, "No, no, you're fine." But it was that day, seeing the way she jumped, seeing the *terror* that crossed her face, when he guessed that she must have been beaten at home. She would have to have been, in order to be so scared at the opening of a door. After he realized this, he took more notice of her, and there were days he saw what seemed to be a bruise, yellow or bluish, on her neck or her arms. He told his wife about it, and Shirley said, "What should we do, Tommy?" And he thought about it, and she thought about it, and they decided they would do nothing.

But the day they discussed this was the day Tommy told his wife what he had seen Ken Barton, Lucy's father, do, years before when Tommy had his dairy farm and Ken worked on the machinery at times. Tommy had walked out behind one of the barns and seen Ken Barton with his pants down by his ankles, pulling on himself, swearing—what a thing to have come upon! Tommy said, "None of that out here, Ken," and the man turned around and got into his truck and drove off, and he did not return to work for a week.

"Tommy, why didn't you tell me this?" Shirley's blue eyes looked up at him with horror.

And Tommy said it seemed too awful to repeat.

"Tommy, we need to do something," his wife said that day. And they talked about it more, and decided once again there was nothing they could do.

———

The blind moved slightly, and then the door opened, and Pete Barton stood there. "Hello, Tommy," he said. Pete stepped outside into the sunshine, closing the door behind him, and stood next to Tommy, and Tommy understood that Pete didn't want him inside the house; already a rank odor came to Tommy, maybe coming off Pete himself.

"Just driving by, and I thought I'd see how you were doing." Tommy said this casually.

"Thanks, I'm okay. Thank you." In the bright sun Pete's face looked pale, and his hair was almost all gray now, but it was a pale gray, and it seemed to match the pale shingles of the house he stood in front of.

"You're working over at the Darr place?" Tommy asked.

Pete said he was, though that job was almost done, but he had another lined up in Hanston.

"Good." Tommy squinted toward the horizon, all soybean fields in front of him, the bright green of them showing in the brown soil. Right on the horizon was the barn of the Pederson place.

They spoke of different machines then, and also of the wind turbines that had been put up recently between Carlisle and Hanston. "We've just got to get used to them, I guess," said Tommy. And Pete said he guessed Tommy was right about that. The one tree that stood next to the driveway had its little leaves out, and the branches dipped for a moment in the wind.

Pete leaned against Tommy's car, his arms folded across his chest. He was a tall man, but his chest seemed almost concave, he was that thin. "Were you in the war, Tommy?"

Tommy was surprised at the question. "No," he said. "No, I was too young, just missed it. My older brother was, though." Up and down quickly, once, went the branches of the tree, as though it had felt a breeze that Tommy had not.

"Where was he?"

Tommy hesitated. Then he said, "He was assigned to the camps, at the end of the war, he was in the corps that went to the camps in Buchenwald." Tommy looked up at the sky, reached into his pocket, pulled out his sunglasses and slipped them onto his face. "He was changed after that. I can't say how, but he was changed." He walked over and leaned against his car, next to Pete.

After a moment, Pete Barton turned toward Tommy. In a voice without belligerence, even with a touch of apology to it, he said, "Look, Tommy. I'd like it if you didn't keep coming over here." Pete's lips were pale and cracked, and he wet them with his tongue, looking at the ground. For a moment Tommy was not sure he heard right, but as he started to say "I only—" Pete looked at him fleetingly and said, "You do it to torture me, and I think enough time has gone by now."

Tommy pushed himself away from the car and stood straight, looking through his sunglasses at Pete. "Torture you?" Tommy asked. "Pete, I'm not here to torture you."

A sudden small gust of wind blew up the road then, and

the dirt they stood on swirled a tiny bit. Tommy took his sunglasses off so that Pete could see his eyes; he looked at him with great concern.

"Forget I said that, I'm sorry." Pete's head ducked down.

"I just like to check on you every so often," Tommy said. "You know, neighbor to neighbor. You live here all alone. Seems to me a neighbor should check in once in a while."

Pete looked at Tommy with a wry smile and said, "Well, you're the only man who ever does that. Or woman." Pete laughed; it was an uncomfortable sound.

They stood, the two of them, Tommy's arms unfolded now; he slipped his hands into his pockets, and Pete slipped his hands into his pockets as well. Pete kicked at a stone, then turned to look out over the field. "The Pedersons should take that tree away, I don't know why they don't. It was one thing to plow around it when it was standing up straight, but now, sheesh."

"They're going to, I heard them talking." Tommy did not quite know what to do, and this was an odd feeling for him.

Still looking toward the toppled tree, Pete said, "My father was in the war. He got all screwed up." Now Pete turned and looked at Tommy, his eyes squinting in the sunshine. "When he was dying he told me about it. It was terrible what happened to him, and then—then he shot these two German guys, he knew they weren't soldiers, they were almost kids, but he told me he felt every day of his life that he should have killed himself in return."

Tommy listened to this, looking at the boy—the man—without his sunglasses, which he held in his hand in his pocket. "I'm sorry," he said. "I didn't know your father was in the war."

"My father—" And here Pete unmistakably had tears in his eyes. "My father was a *decent* man, Tommy."

Tommy nodded slowly.

"He did things because he couldn't control himself. And so he—" Pete turned away. In a moment he turned partway back to Tommy and said, "And so he went in and turned on those milking machines that night, and then the place burned down, and I never, ever forgot it, Tommy, it was like I *knew* he had done it. And I know you know that too."

Tommy felt his scalp break out into goosebumps. It continued, he felt the bumps crawling across his head. The sun seemed very bright, and yet it seemed it shone in a cone around only him. In a moment he said, "Son"—the word came out involuntarily—"you mustn't think that."

"Look," Pete said, and his face had some color to it now. "He knew the milking machines could cause trouble—he'd talked about it. He'd said it wasn't a very sophisticated system and they could get overheated in a hurry."

Tommy said, "He was right about that."

"He was mad at you. He was always mad at someone, but he was mad at you. I don't know what happened, but he was working at your place, and then he stopped. I think he went back eventually, but he never liked you after whatever happened had happened."

Tommy put his sunglasses back on. He said with deliberateness, "I found him playing with himself, Pete, pulling on himself, behind the barns, and I said that was something he couldn't do there."

"Oh, man." Pete wiped at his nose. "Oh, man." He looked up at the sky. Then he looked at Tommy quickly and said, "Well, he didn't like you. And the night before the fire, he went out—sometimes he would just do that, go out, he wasn't a drinker, but sometimes he'd just leave the house and go out, and that night he went out and he got back around midnight, I remember because my sister couldn't sleep, she was too cold, and my mother—" Here Pete stopped, as though to catch his breath. "Well, my mother was up with her, and I remember she said, Lucy go to *sleep*, it's midnight! And my father came home. And the next morning when I was at school— Well, we all heard about the fire. And I just knew."

Tommy steadied himself against the car. He said nothing.

"And you knew too," Pete finally said. "And that's why you stop by here, to torture me."

For many moments, the two men stood there. The breeze had picked up and Tommy felt it ripple the sleeves of his shirt. Then Pete turned to go back inside the house; the door opened with a squeak. "Pete," Tommy called. "Pete, listen to me. I don't come here to torture you. And I still don't know—even with what you just told me—that it's true."

Pete turned back; after a moment he closed the door behind him and walked back to Tommy. His eyes were moist, either from the wind that was whipping up or from tears, Tommy didn't know. Pete spoke almost tiredly. "I'm just telling you, Tommy. He wasn't supposed to go and do those things in the war that he had to do. People aren't *supposed* to murder people. And he did, and he did awful things, and awful things happened to him, and he couldn't live *inside* himself, Tommy. That's what I'm trying to say. Other men could do it, but he couldn't, it ruined him, and—"

"What about your mother?" Tommy asked suddenly.

Pete's face changed; a blankness of expression came to it. "What about her?" he asked.

"How did she take all this?"

Pete seemed defeated by this question. He shook his head slowly. "I don't know," he said. "I don't know what my mother was like."

"I never really knew her myself," Tommy said. "Just saw her out and about once in a while." But it came to him now: He had never seen the woman smile.

Pete was gazing at the ground. He shrugged and said, "I don't know about my mother."

Tommy's mind, which had been spinning, rearranged itself; he felt himself again. "Now listen, Pete. I'm glad you told me about your father being in the war. I heard what you said. You said he was a decent man, and I believe you."

"But he *was*!" Pete almost wailed this, looking at Tommy with his pale eyes. "Whenever he did something, he felt terrible about it later, and after your fire he was so—so *agitated*, Tommy, for weeks and weeks he was worse than ever."

"It's okay, Pete."

"But it's *not*."

"But it is." Tommy said this firmly. He walked over to the man and put his hand on Pete's arm for a moment. Then he added, "And I don't think he did it, anyway. I think I forgot to turn the machines off that night, and your father was mad at me, and he probably felt bad about what happened. He never told you he did it, am I right? When he was dying, and told you about killing those men in the war, he never confessed to burning my barns down. Did he?"

Pete shook his head.

"Then I suggest you let it go, Pete. You've had enough to contend with."

Pete ran a hand over his hair, a piece of it stood up briefly. With some confusion he said, "Contend with?"

"I saw how you were treated by the town, Pete. And your sisters, too. I saw that when I was a janitor." Tommy felt slightly winded.

Pete gave a small shrug. He still seemed vaguely confused. "Okay," he said. "Okay, then."

They stood a few more moments in the breeze and then Tommy said he was going to get going. "Hold on," said Pete. "Let me drive down the road with you. It's time I got rid of that sign of my mother's. I've been meaning to do that, and I'll do it now. Hold on," he said again. Tommy waited by the car while Pete went inside the house, and very soon Pete came back out, holding a sledgehammer. Tommy got in the driver's seat, and Pete got in on the passenger's side, and together they drove down the road; the rank odor Tommy had smelled before was stronger now with the man next to him. As he drove, Tommy suddenly remembered how one time he had put a quarter near the desk where Lucy would sit when she was in junior high school. She always went to Mr. Haley's room; the man taught Social Studies for a year, then went into the service, but he must have been kind to Lucy because that was the room, even when it later became the science room, that Lucy preferred to be in. And so one day Tommy left a quarter near the desk he knew she sat at. The school had just gotten a vending machine and there were ice cream sandwiches you could buy for a quarter, so he left the quarter there where Lucy could see it. That night, after she had gone home, Tommy went into the room and the quarter was still there, exactly where he had left it.

He almost asked Pete, then, about Lucy, if they were in touch, but he had already pulled up next to the sign that said SEWING AND ALTERATIONS and so he just said, "Here you go, Pete. You be well." And Pete thanked him and got out of the car.

After a few moments, Tommy glanced in his rearview mirror, and what he saw was Pete Barton hitting the sign with the sledgehammer. Something about the way he hit it—the force—made Tommy watch carefully as he drove down the road. He saw the boy—the man—hit the sign again and again with what seemed to be increasing force, and as Tommy's car dipped down just slightly, losing sight for a moment, he thought: Wait. And when his car came back up he looked again in the rearview mirror and he saw again this boy-man hitting that sign with rage, with a ferocity that astonished Tommy, it was astonishing, the rage with which that man was hitting that sign. It seemed indecent to Tommy that he was witnessing it, for it felt as private in its anguish as what the boy's father had been doing out behind Tommy's barns that day. And then as Tommy drove he realized: Oh, it was the mother. It was the mother. She must have been the really dangerous one.

He slowed the car, then turned it around. As he drove back, he saw that Pete had stopped smashing the sign, and was now kicking at the pieces with a tired dejection. Pete looked up, surprise showing on his face, as Tommy approached. Tommy leaned to unroll the passenger's window and said, "Pete, get in." The man hesitated, sweat on his face now. "Get in," Tommy said again.

Pete got back into the car and Tommy drove down the road, back to the Barton home. He turned the car engine off. "Pete, I want you to listen to me very, very carefully."

A look of fear passed over Pete's face, and Tommy put his hand briefly on the man's knee. It was the look of terror that had passed over Lucy's face when he surprised her in the classroom. "I want to tell you something I had never in my life planned on telling anyone. But on the night of the fire—" And Tommy told him then, in detail, how he had felt God come to him, and how God had let Tommy know it was all okay. When he was done, Pete, who had listened intently, sometimes looking down, sometimes looking at Tommy, now looked at Tommy with wonder on his face.

"So you believe that?" Pete asked.

"I don't believe it," Tommy said. "I know it."

"And you never even told your wife?"

"I never did, no."

"But why not?"

"I guess there are some things in life we don't tell others."

Pete looked down at his hands, and Tommy looked at the man's hands as well. He was surprised by them, they were strong-fingered, large; they were a grown man's hands.

"So you're saying my father was doing God's work." Pete shook his head slowly.

"No, I'm telling you what happened to me that night."

"I know. I hear what you're telling me." Pete gazed through the windshield. "I just don't know what to make of it."

Tommy looked at the truck that sat next to the house; its fender glinted in the sunlight. The truck was old and gray-brown. It almost matched the color of the house. It seemed to Tommy that he sat there for many minutes looking at that truck and how it matched the house.

"Tell me how Lucy is," said Tommy then, moving his feet, hearing them scrape over the grit on the floor of the car. "I saw she's got a new book."

"She's good," said Pete, and his face lit up. "She's good, and it's a good book, she sent me an early copy. I'm really proud of her."

Tommy said, "You know, she wouldn't even take a quarter I left her once," and he told Pete about leaving the quarter and finding it later.

"No, Lucy wouldn't have taken a penny that wasn't hers," Pete said. He added, "My sister Vicky, well, she's another story. I bet she would have taken the quarter and then asked for more." He glanced at Tommy. "Yeah. She'd have taken it."

"Well, I guess there's always that struggle between what to do and what not to do," Tommy said, attempting to be jocular.

Pete said, "What?" And Tommy repeated it.

"That's interesting," said Pete, and Tommy was struck with a sense of being with a child, not a grown man, and he looked again at Pete's hands.

The car engine made a few clicking sounds as they sat in silence. "You asked about my mother," Pete said after a few moments. "Nobody has ever asked me about my mother. But the truth is, I don't know if my mother loved us or not. I don't know about her in some big way." He looked at Tommy, and Tommy nodded. "But my father loved us,"

Pete said. "I know he did. He was troubled, oh, man, was he troubled. But he loved us."

Tommy nodded his head again.

"Tell me more about what you just said," Pete asked.

"About what? What was I just saying?"

"The—struggle, did you say that? Between doing what we should and what we shouldn't do."

"Oh." Tommy looked through the windshield at the house sitting so silently and so worn out there in the sunshine, its blinds drawn like tired eyelids. "Well, here's an example on a large scale." And then Tommy told Pete about what his brother had seen in the war, the women who had walked through the camps, how some had wept and others had looked furious and would not be made to feel bad. "And so there's a struggle, or a contest, I guess you could say, all the time, it seems to me. And remorse, well, to be able to show remorse—to be able to be sorry about what we've done that's hurt other people—that keeps us human." Tommy put his hand on the steering wheel. "That's what I think," he said.

"My father showed remorse. He's what you're talking about, in one person. The contest."

"I suppose you're right."

The sun had grown so high in the sky it could not be seen from the car.

"I never have talks like this," said Pete, and Tommy was struck once again by how young this boy-man seemed.

Tommy experienced a tiny physical pain deep in his chest that seemed directly connected to Pete.

"I'm an old man," said Tommy. "I think if we're going to have talks like this one I should stop by more often. How about I see you two Saturdays from now?"

Tommy was surprised to see Pete's hands become fists that he banged down on his knees. "No," Pete said. "No. You don't have to. No."

"I want to," said Tommy, and he thought—then he knew—as he said this that it was not true. But did that matter? It didn't matter.

"I don't need someone coming to see me out of obligation." Pete said this quietly.

The pain deep in Tommy's chest increased. "I don't blame you for that," he said. They sat together in the car, which was now warm, and the smell, to Tommy, was palpable.

In a moment Pete spoke again, "Well, I guess I thought you were coming here to torture me, and I was wrong about that. So I guess maybe I'd be wrong to think you were just obliging me."

"I think you'd be wrong," said Tommy. But he was aware, again, that this was not true. The truth was that he did not really want to visit this poor boy-man seated next to him ever again.

They sat in silence for a few moments more; then Pete turned to Tommy, gave him a nod. "All right, I'll see you

then," said Pete, getting out of the car. "Thanks, Tommy,"
he said, and Tommy said, "Thank *you*."

*

Driving home, Tommy was aware of a sensation like that
of a tire becoming flat, as though he had been filled—all his
life—with some sustaining air, and it was gone now; he felt,
increasingly as he drove, a sense of fear. He could not understand it. But he had told what he had vowed to himself
never to tell—that God had come to him the night of the
fire. Why had he told? Because he wanted to give something
to that poor boy who had been smashing the sign of his
mother so ferociously. Why did it matter that he had told
the boy? Tommy wasn't sure. But Tommy felt he had pulled
the plug on himself, that by telling the thing he would never
tell he had diminished himself past forgiveness. It really
frightened him. *So you believe that?*, Pete Barton had said.

He felt no longer himself.

He said, quietly, "God, what have I done?" And he meant
that he was really asking God. And then he said, "Where
are you, God?" But the car remained the same, warm, still
slightly smelling from the presence of Pete Barton, just
rumbling over the road.

He drove more quickly than he usually did. Going past
him were the fields of soybeans and corn and the brown
fields as well, and he saw them only barely.

At home, Shirley was sitting on the front steps; her glasses twinkled in the sunlight, and she waved to him as he drove up the small driveway. "Shirley," he called as he got out of the car. "Shirley." She pulled herself up from the steps by holding on to the railing, and came to him with worry on her face. "Shirley," he said, "I have to tell you about something."

At the small kitchen table, in their small kitchen, they sat. A tall water glass held peony buds, and Shirley pushed it to the side. Tommy told her then what had just happened that morning at the Barton home, and she kept shaking her head, pushing her glasses up her nose with the back of her hand. "Oh, Tommy," she said. "Oh, that poor boy."

"But here's the thing, Shirley. It's more than that. There's something else I need to tell you."

And so Tommy looked at his wife—her blue eyes behind her glasses, a faded blue these days, but with the tiny shiny parts from her cataract surgery—and he told her then, with the same detail he had told Pete Barton, how he had felt God come to him the night of the fire. "But now I think I must have imagined it," Tommy said. "It couldn't have happened, I made it up." He opened both his hands upward, shook his head.

His wife watched him for a moment; he saw her watching him, saw her eyes get a little bit bigger then begin to break into a tenderness around their corners. She leaned forward, took his hand, and said, "But, Tommy. Why couldn't it have happened? Why couldn't it have been just what you thought it was that night?"

And then Tommy understood: that what he had kept from her their whole lives was, in fact, easily acceptable to her, and what he would keep from her now—his doubt (his sudden belief that God had never come to him)—was a new secret replacing the first. He took his hand from hers. "You might be right," he said. A paltry thing he added, but it was true: He said, "I love you, Shirley." And then he looked at the ceiling; he could not look at her for a moment or two.

Windmills

A few years ago, with morning sunlight coming into her bedroom, Patty Nicely had had the television on, and the sunlight had caused whatever was on the screen to be unseen from certain angles. Patty's husband, Sebastian, was still alive then, and she was getting herself ready for work. Earlier, she had been making sure that he was set for the day; his illness had only begun back then and she was not sure—they were not sure—what the final outcome would be. On the television was the usual morning show, and Patty watched intermittently as she moved about the bedroom. She was sticking a pearl earring into her earlobe when she heard the woman announcer saying, "Lucy Barton will be with us after the break."

Patty walked toward the television and squinted, and in a few minutes Lucy Barton—who had written a novel—came on and Patty said, "Oh my gosh." She went to the bedroom

door and called, "Sibby?" Sebastian came into the bedroom
then, and Patty said, "Oh, honey, oh, Sibby." She helped him
into bed, and smoothed his forehead. The reason she remembered this now—the fact that Lucy Barton had been on
television—was because she had then told Sebastian about
the woman. Lucy Barton had grown up terribly poor, right
nearby in Amgash, Illinois. "I didn't know them, since I was
in school in Hanston, but they were the kids that people
would say, Oh, cooties!, and run away from," she explained
to her husband. Here was why Patty knew this: Lucy's
mother had made dresses, and Patty's mother had used her
as a seamstress. A few times, Patty's mother had taken Patty
and her sisters to Lucy Barton's home. The place the Bar-
tons lived in was tiny, and it *smelled*! But here was Lucy Barton: Why, she had become a writer and was living in New
York City. Patty said, "Look, honey, she looks nice."

Sebastian had become interested; she saw his keenness
as he listened to this story. In a few minutes he asked some
questions, for example, had Lucy seemed different from her
brother and sister? Patty said she didn't know; she hadn't
known any of them, really. *But*—here was something odd:
Lucy's parents had been asked to the wedding of Patty's
oldest sister, Linda, and Patty had never figured that out,
she couldn't imagine Lucy's father had even owned a suit,
why would they have been at her sister's wedding? Sebastian said, Maybe your mother didn't have anyone else who
would talk to her at that point, and Patty realized he was
exactly right. Patty's face had turned bright red as she saw

the truth to this. Sweetheart, said Sebastian, and reached for her hand.

A few months later Sebastian was gone. Having met in their late thirties, they'd had only eight years together. No children. Patty had never known a better man.

※

Today she drove with her car's air conditioner turned on high; her extra weight made Patty get hot easily, and it was already late May and the weather was lovely—everyone kept saying that the weather was lovely—but for Patty that meant it was really too warm. She drove by a field where the corn was just inches high, and by a field of soybeans bright green and close to the ground. Then she drove through the town, winding her way around the street where some of the houses had explosions of peonies by their porches—Patty loved peonies—and then to the school where she was a high school guidance counselor. She parked, checked her lipstick in the rearview mirror, gave her hair a bounce with her hand, then heaved herself from the car. Across the parking lot was Angelina Mumford getting out of her own car; she was a middle school Social Studies teacher, and her husband had recently left her. Patty gave a big wave, and Angelina waved back.

In Patty's office were many folders, and also a cluster of small-framed photographs of her nieces and nephews, and there were pamphlets from colleges, all in an array on top

of her filing cabinet and on her desk. And there was her
scheduling book on her desk too. Lila Lane had missed her
appointment from the day before. There was a knock on
the door—which was open—and a tall, pretty girl stood
there. "Come in," Patty said. "Lila?"

Unease came into the room with the girl. She slouched in
her chair, and the glance she gave Patty made Patty frightened. The girl's hair was long and blond, and as she reached
to pull it up and across one shoulder, Patty saw the tattoos—
like a small barbed wire fence—that went across the girl's
wrist. Patty said, "That's a nice name, Lila Lane." The girl
said, "I was supposed to be named for my aunt, but at the
last minute my mom said, Fuck her."

Patty took the papers and bounced their edges against
her desk.

The girl sat up straight, and spoke with suddenness.
"She's a bitch. She thinks she's better than any of us. I never
even *met* her."

"You never met your aunt?"

"Nope. She came back here when her father died, my
mother's father, and then she went away and I've never met
her. She lives in New York and she thinks her shit doesn't
stink."

"Well, let's look at your scores here. These are pretty
good scores." Patty never liked her students to speak
roughly; she found it disrespectful. She looked over at the
girl, then back at the papers. "Your grades are good, too,"
Patty added.

"I skipped third grade." The girl said this with a tone of belligerence, but Patty thought she heard the pride beneath it.

Patty said, "Good for you. Well, then, I guess you were always a good student. They don't let you skip a grade for nothing." She raised her eyebrows pleasantly at the girl, but Lila was looking around Patty's office, studying the pamphlets, the photos of Patty's nieces and nephews, and then finally she looked for a long moment at the poster on the wall that had a kitten swinging from a branch with the block letters HANG IN THERE below the kitten.

Lila looked back at Patty. "What?" she said.

"I said, they don't let you skip a grade for nothing," Patty repeated.

"Of course they don't. Jeeze-lew-*eeze*." The girl moved her long legs so that they went in the other direction, but she stayed slouching.

"Okay." Patty nodded. "So what about your future? You have good grades, good scores—"

"Are these your kids?" The girl was squinting, and she pointed laconically at the photos.

"Those are my nieces and nephews," Patty said.

"I know you don't have kids," the girl said with a smirk. "How come you don't have kids?"

Patty felt the faintest blush come to her face. "It just never happened. Now let's talk about your future."

"'Cause you never did it with your husband?" The girl laughed; her teeth were bad. "That's what people say, you know. Fatty Patty never did it with her husband, *Igor,* never did it with anyone. People say you're a virgin."

Patty put the papers flat down on the desk. She could feel her face become flaming hot. For a moment her vision blurred; she heard the ticking of the clock on the wall. In her wildest dreams she could not have anticipated what was going to come out of her mouth. She looked hard at the girl and heard herself say the words "Get out of here right now, you piece of filth."

The girl seemed stunned for just a moment, but then she said, "Hey, *wow.* They're right. Oh my God!" And covering her mouth she made a sound of laughter that grew in length and depth so that Patty had a sense of it spilling from her mouth like bile from some creature in a horror film. "Sorry," the girl said in a moment. "Sorry."

From nowhere Patty suddenly knew who the girl was. "Your aunt is Lucy Barton," Patty said. She added, "You look like her."

The girl stood up and left the room.

Patty closed the door to her office and telephoned her sister Linda, who lived outside of Chicago. Perspiration made Patty's face moist, and she felt her underarms sticky with it.

Her sister answered, saying, "Linda Peterson-Cornell."

"It's me," Patty said.

"I figured. The phone said your school's name."

"Well, then how come— Listen, Linda." And she told

her sister what had just happened. Patty spoke in a rush, leaving out what she had said to the girl. "Can you believe it?" she finished. She heard her sister sigh. After a moment, Linda said she never understood how Patty could work with adolescents anyway. Patty told her she was missing the point.

Linda said, "No, I'm not missing the point. The point is Lila Lane, Lucy Barton, Lila this, Lucy that. But who cares about them?" When there was a pause, Linda continued, "Seriously, Patty. The fact that Lucy Barton's niece is such trash should come as no surprise, I mean really."

"Why do you say that?"

"Because. Don't you remember them? They were just *trash*, Patty. Oh my God, I just remembered they had those—what? Cousins, I think? The boy's name was Abel. Oh my God, he was something. He'd stand in the dumpster behind Chatwin's Cake Shoppe and go through the garbage, looking for stuff to eat. Was he *that* hungry? Why would he do that? But I remember he'd do it with no embarrassment at all. I remember Lucy being with him. It made me shudder. It still does, honestly. His sister's name was Dottie. A scrawny girl. Dottie and Abel Blaine. It's kind of amazing I remember them. But how could I forget? I'd never before seen anyone going through garbage looking for something to eat. He was a handsome kid too."

"Gosh," Patty said. The heat from her face had started to go away. She asked, "Didn't Lucy's parents come to your wedding? Your first one."

"I don't remember," Linda said.

"You do so remember. How come they came to your *wedding?*"

"Because she invited them, to have people there who would speak to her. For God's sake, Patty. Just forget that. I have."

Patty said, "Well, maybe you've forgotten, but you still have his name. Peterson. After only a year of being married to him."

Linda said, "And why in the world would I want the name Nicely back? I never understood why you kept it yourself. The Pretty Nicely Girls. How *horrible* that we were known as the Pretty Nicely Girls."

Patty thought: It wasn't horrible.

Linda added, "Have you seen Our Mother who is not yet in Heaven recently? How's her dippiness factor these days?"

Patty said, "I thought I'd go out there this afternoon. It's been a few days. I need to make sure she's taking her medicine."

"I don't care if she takes it," Linda said, and Patty said she knew that.

Then Patty said, "Are you in a bad mood or anything?"

"No, I'm not," Linda said.

＊

It was a Friday, and in town that afternoon, Patty went to the bank with her paycheck, and then walking down the sidewalk she looked into the bookstore and saw—placed right in the front of the display—a new book by Lucy Barton. "My gosh," Patty said. Inside the bookstore was Charlie Macauley, and Patty almost walked out when she saw him because he was the only man, other than Sebastian, that she loved. She really loved him. She had liked him for years without knowing him too well, the way people in small towns know one another but don't know one another too. At Sibby's funeral, when she turned and saw him alone in the back row, she fell—fell—head over heels in love with him, and she had been in love with him since. He was with his grandson, a boy in elementary school, and when Charlie looked up and saw Patty, his face opened, and he nodded. "Hi, Charlie," she said, and then she asked the bookstore owner about the book by Lucy Barton.

It was a memoir.

A memoir? Patty picked it up and glanced through it, though the words bounced around because of Charlie being so close by. Patty took the book to the register and bought it. She glanced at Charlie on her way out, and he gave her a wave. Charlie Macauley was old enough to be her father, though he was younger than her father would have been if he had still been alive. But Charlie was at least twenty years older than Patty; he had been in the Vietnam war when he was young. How Patty knew this, she could not have said. His wife was notably plain, and thin as a stick.

———

Patty's house was a few streets away from the center of
town. It was not a big house, but it was not a small house
either. She and Sibby had bought it together and it had a
front porch and a small side porch too. Her peonies were
heavy-headed by the side porch and there were irises now in
bloom as well. Through her kitchen window she could see
the irises as she took a box of cookies from the cupboard—
they were Nilla Wafers and the box was half full—and then
she went into her living room and sat down and ate every
one. Then she went back to the kitchen and had a glass of
milk. She telephoned her mother to say she would be over
in an hour or so, and her mother said, "Oh, *goodie.*"

Upstairs, sunlight came through the windows and spilled
into the hallway. Little dust bunnies were gathered up and
down the floor. "Oh dear," Patty said. She said that a few
times, sitting on her bed. "Oh dear, oh dear," she said.

It was a twenty-mile ride to the town of Hanston, and
the sun was still bright as Patty drove by the fields, some
with the little plants of corn, some brown, one field was
being plowed under as she drove by. Then she came to the
place where there were wind turbines, over a hundred of
them along the horizon, these huge white windmills that
had been put up across the land almost ten years earlier.
They fascinated Patty, they always had, their long white
arms twirling the air all at the same speed but otherwise
without synchronicity. There was a lawsuit now, she remembered, there were often lawsuits, about the destruction
of birds and deer and farmland, but Patty favored the large

white things whose skinny arms moved against the sky in that slightly wacky way to make energy—and then they were behind her, and once again were only the fields with the little corn plants and the fresh bright soybeans. These were the very cornfields—in their summer fullness—where, by the age of fifteen, she had allowed boys to thrust themselves against her, their lips huge-seeming, rubbery, their things bulging through their pants, and she would gasp and offer her neck to be kissed and grind herself against them, but—really?—she couldn't stand it she couldn't stand it she couldn't stand it.

Patty came into the town that had changed very little since she had grown up there. There were the old-fashioned-looking streetlamps, black, with their lights in a box at the top. And there were the two restaurants, the gift shop, the investment firm, the clothing store—all had the same green awnings and signs in black and white. In order to get to her mother's house she had to drive past the home she had grown up in, a beautiful red house with black shutters and a wide porch with a porch swing on it. Patty had sat on that swing with her mother for hours at a time as a young child, curled against her mother's stomach, crumpling the fabric of her mother's dress, her mother's laughter above her head. Her father had lived in that house until he died, which had been one year before Sibby died. Now a family with lots of children owned the house, and Patty always—every single time she drove by it—looked the other way. Through the town and just a mile past was her mother's small white house. As Patty turned in to the driveway, she saw her mother peering through the front curtain, then could hear her cane thump against the floor as Patty unlocked the side door and let herself in. Her mother had become as little as Patty had become big. This is what Patty thought each time she saw her mother now. "Hey," Patty said, and stooped, and kissed the air beside her mother. Standing straight, she said, "I brought you some food."

"I don't need food." Her mother had on a terrycloth bathrobe, and she gave the belt a tug.

Patty unpacked the meatloaf and the coleslaw and the mashed potatoes, and put them in the refrigerator. "You need to eat something," Patty said.

"I won't eat anything sitting alone. Can you stay and eat with me?" Her mother looked up at her through her large glasses, which had slipped partway down her nose. "Pretty please?" Patty closed her eyes briefly, then nodded.

As Patty set the table, her mother sat in a chair, her legs apart beneath the robe, looking up at Patty. "It's awfully good to see you. I never see you anymore."

"I was here three days ago," Patty said. Her mother's thin hair—the scalp so visible—stayed in Patty's mind as she turned toward the counter, and inside she felt herself crumble. Returning to the table, pulling a chair up, she said, "We have to talk about you going into the Golden Leaf. Remember we talked about that?" Confusion seemed to appear on her mother's face; she shook her head slowly. "Did you get dressed today?" Patty asked.

Her mother looked down at the lap of her bathrobe and then up at Patty once more. "No," she said.

✳

At a conference in St. Louis, Patty had met her husband. The conference was on dealing with children from low-income homes, but Sebastian was not part of that. He was staying in the hotel room next to Patty's; there for a conference himself, he was a mechanical engineer. "Hello again!" Patty had said as they both stepped from their rooms. She had seen him at night going into his room when she went into hers. What it was about him, she could not have said, but he made her feel completely comfortable; she was already gaining weight from her antidepressants, and she had once stopped a wedding from happening only weeks before she was to be married. Sebastian would not even look at her the first few times they spoke. But he was a nice-looking man, tall, thin, his face was gaunt, his hair on the longer side. His eyebrows were so thick they were like one line across his forehead, his eyes indented beneath his brow. She just *liked* him. And by the end of the conference she had obtained his email address, and their correspondence was something she'd never forget. Within just a few weeks he wrote, *There's something you should know about me, Patty, if we're going to be friends.* And then a few days later: *Things happened to me,* he wrote. *Awful things. They've made me different from other people.* He lived in Missouri, and when she wrote and asked him to come to Carlisle, Illinois, she was surprised that he agreed. After that, they were together. How had she known—she hadn't known—that he had been taken as a boy again and again and again by his stepfather? Sebastian could hardly stand being with people, but it was very early on that he looked at her and told her in some detail what had happened to him, and he said to her, Patty, I love you, but I cannot *do it*. I just cannot do *that*, I wish I could. And she said, "That's okay, I can't stand it either."

In their marriage bed they held hands, and never went any further. Often, during the first years especially, he had terrible dreams, and he would kick the covers and squeal, it was a frightening sound. She noticed that he was aroused when this happened, and she was always sure to touch only his shoulders until he calmed down. Then she rubbed his forehead. "It's okay, honey," she always said. He would stare at the ceiling, his hands in fists. Thank you, he said. Turning his face toward her, Thank you, Patty, he said.

"Tell me, tell me. Smell me. How are you?" Her mother poked a forkful of meatloaf into her mouth.

"I'm well. I'm going to see Angelina tomorrow night. Her husband's left her." Patty put mashed potatoes on her meatloaf, then put butter on the mashed potatoes.

"I don't know who you're talking about." Her mother placed her fork on the table and looked at her quizzically.

"Angelina, she's one of the Mumford girls."

"Huh." Her mother nodded slowly. "Oh, I know. Her mother was Mary Mumford. Sure. She wasn't much."

"Who wasn't much? Angelina's a great person. I always thought her mother was really nice."

"Oh, she was *nice*. She just wasn't much. I think she came from Mississippi originally. She married that Mumford boy, he was rich, and then she had all those girls and plenty of money."

Patty opened her mouth. She was going to ask if her mother remembered that Mary Mumford had left that rich husband only a few years ago, in her seventies, did she remember that? But Patty wouldn't ask. She would not tell her mother that she and Angelina had become friends over it: *mothers leaving.*

I wanted to kill him, Sebastian had told Patty. I really did want to kill him. "Of course you did," she had said. And I wanted to kill my mother too, he said. And Patty said, "Of course you did."

Patty looked around her mother's small kitchen. It was spotless, thanks to Olga, a woman older than Patty who came in twice a week. But the table she sat at had a linoleum top that was cracked at the corners, and the curtains at the window were very faded in their blue. And Patty could see from where she sat, down the hallway to the corner of the living room, the blue beanbag chair that her mother, after all these years, refused to give up.

Her mother was talking—so often this was the case these days—of things from the past. "All those dances at The Club. My goodness, they were fun." Her mother paused to shake her head with wonder.

Patty put another slab of butter on her potatoes, ate the potatoes, and then pushed the plate aside. "Lucy Barton's written a memoir," she said.

Her mother said, "What did you say?" And Patty repeated it.

"Now I remember," her mother said. "They used to live in a garage, and then the old man died—whatever relative he was, I have no idea—but they moved into the house."

"A garage? Is that where I remember going? A *garage*?"

Her mother said, after a moment, "I don't know, I can't remember, but she was very inexpensive, that's why I used her. She did wonderful work really, and she barely charged a nickel for it." After a long moment, her mother said, "I saw Lucy on TV a few years ago. Hot shot. She wrote a book or something. Lives in New York. Smork. La-de-dah."

Patty took a deep, unquiet breath. Her mother reached for the coleslaw, and as her bathrobe fell open slightly, Patty could see—briefly—the flattened small breast beneath the nightgown. After a few minutes Patty stood up, cleared the table, and did the dishes rapidly. "Let's check your meds," she said, and her mother waved a hand dismissively. So

Patty went into the bathroom and found the container with the divided daily sections, and saw that her mother had not taken any of the pills since Patty was last there. Patty brought the container out to her mother and explained again why each pill was important, and her mother said, "All right." She took the pills that Patty handed her. "You need to take these," Patty told her. "You don't want to have a stroke." She did not say anything about the medicine that was supposed to slow dementia.

"I'm not going to have a stroke. Stroke poke."

"Okay, I'll see you soon."

"You turned out the best," her mother said at the door. "It's too bad your be-happy pills added that weight, but you're still pretty. Are you sure you have to go?"

Walking down the driveway to her car, Patty said out loud, "Oh my gosh."

❋

The sun had just set, and by the time Patty was halfway home—past the windmills—the full moon was starting to rise. The night her father died the moon was full, and in Patty's mind every time the moon became full she felt that her father was watching her. She wiggled her fingers from the steering wheel as a hello to him. Love you, Daddy, she whispered. And she meant Sibby as well, for they had merged, in a way, in her mind. They were up there watching her, and she knew that the moon was just a rock—a rock!—

but the sight of its fullness always made her feel that her men were out there, up there, too. Wait for me, she whispered. Because she knew—she almost knew—that when she died she would be with her father and Sibby again. Thank you, she whispered, because her father had just told her it was good of her to take care of her mother. He was generous now in this way; death had given that to him.

At home, the lights she'd left on made her house appear cozy; it was one of many things she had learned about living alone, leaving lights on. And yet as she put her pocketbook down, moved through the living room, the ghastliness descended; her day had been a bad one. Lila Lane had shaken her profoundly, and what if the girl reported her, told the principal that Patty had called her a piece of filth? She could do that, Lila Lane. She was up to doing that. Patty's sister had been no help, there was no point in calling her other sister, who lived in L.A. and never had time to talk, and her mother—oh, her mother . . .

"Fatty Patty." Patty said these words aloud.

Patty sat down on her couch and looked around; the house seemed faintly unfamiliar, and this was—she had learned—a bad sign. A taste of meatloaf was in her mouth. "Fatty Patty, you get yourself ready for the night," she said out loud, and she rose, and flossed her teeth and then brushed them, and washed her face; she put her face cream on, and this made her feel just a little bit better. When she looked into her pocketbook to find her phone, she saw the small book by Lucy Barton that she had slipped in there

earlier. She sat down and examined the cover. It showed a
city building at dusk with its lights on. Then she began to
read the book. "Holy moley," she said, after a few pages.
"Oh my gosh."

✳

The next morning, Saturday, Patty vacuumed the upstairs
of her house and then the downstairs, she changed the bed,
did the laundry, and she went through the mail, tossing out
the catalogs and flyers. Then Patty went into town and
bought groceries, and she bought some flowers too. It had
been a long time since she had bought flowers for her house.
All day she had the sense of having a piece of yellow-colored
candy, maybe butterscotch, tucked inside the back crevices
of her mouth, and she knew that this private sweetness
came from Lucy Barton's memoir. Every so often Patty
shook her head and said "Huh" aloud.

    In the afternoon she called her mother, and Olga an-
swered. Patty asked her if she could come every day now
instead of two days a week, and Olga said she'd have to
think about it, and Patty said she understood. Then Patty
asked to speak to her mother. "Who is this?" her mother
asked. And Patty said, "It's me, Patty. Your daughter. I love
you, Mom."

    In a moment her mother said, "Well, I love you too."

    After that, Patty had to lie down. She could not have said
the last time she'd told her mother she loved her. As a child

she had said it frequently, she may have even said it that morning when her mother agreed that Patty didn't have to be in Girl Scouts anymore, Patty being a freshman in high school, and her mother said, "Oh, Patty, that's okay, you're old enough now to decide," her mother standing in the kitchen handing her lunch to her in a paper bag, just being herself, Patty's mother. And then Patty had come home from school that same day, in the middle of the day, with cramps—terrible cramps Patty used to have—and Patty came home, and she heard the most astonishing sounds coming from her parents' bedroom. Her mother was crying, gasping, shrieking, and there was the sound of skin being slapped, and Patty had run upstairs and seen her mother astride Mr. Delaney—Patty's Spanish teacher!— and her mother's breasts were swaying and this man was spanking her mother and his mouth reached up and took her mother's breast and her mother wailed. And what Patty never forgot was the look of her mother's eyes, they were wild; her mother could not stop herself from wailing, this is what Patty saw, her mother's breasts and her mother's eyes *looking* at her—yet unable to stop what was coming from her mouth.

Patty had turned and run into her bedroom. After a few minutes, Mr. Delaney's footsteps were heard going down the stairs, and her mother came into her room, a housecoat around her, and her mother said, "Patty, I swear to God you must never tell a soul, and when you're older, you'll understand."

That her mother's breasts were so big Patty would not have imagined, seeing them unharnessed and swinging over that man.

Within days, horrible scenes occurred in a home that had once been so placid and ordinary that Patty had not considered it so. Patty did not, in fact, tell anyone what she had seen—she wouldn't have known what words to use—but she never returned to Mr. Delaney's class, and then—oh, it was so sudden!—her mother, after exploding in a confession, moved into a tiny apartment in town. Patty went to see her there only once, and there was a blue beanbag chair in the corner. The entire town talked of her mother's affair with Mr. Delaney, and to Patty it felt like her head had been cut off and was moving in a different direction from her body. It was the oddest thing, and it went on and on, that feeling. She and her sisters watched as their father wept. They watched as he swore, and became stony-faced. He had been none of these things before, not a weeper, or a swearer, or a stony-faced man. And he became all these things, and the family—they had all just been innocently sitting in a boat on a lake, it seemed like—was gone, turned into something never imagined. The town talked and talked. Patty, being the youngest, had to wait it through the longest. By Christmas, Mr. Delaney had left town, and Patty's mother was alone.

When Patty began to go to the cornfields with the boys

in her class, and even much later, when she had real boy-
friends and she did it with them, there was always the image
of her mother, shirtless, braless, her breasts swaying as that
man grabbed one in his mouth— No, Patty could not stand
any of it. Her own excitement caused her always terrible,
and terrifying, shame.

✳

Angelina was still slim and youthful-looking, although she
was a few years older than Patty. Yet when Patty saw them
both briefly in the mirror at Sam's Place, she thought that
she, Patty, looked much younger—and that Angelina looked
drawn. Right away Patty was going to tell Angelina about
the book by Lucy Barton. But as soon as they sat down,
Angelina's green eyes swam with tears, and Patty reached
across the table and touched her friend's hand. Angelina
held up a finger, and in a minute she was able to speak. "I
just hate *both* of them," she said, and Patty said she understood. "He said to me, 'You're in love with your mother,'
and I was so surprised, Patty, I just stared at him—"

"Oh boy." Patty sighed and sat back.

A few years ago Angelina's mother, at the age of seventy-
four, had left town—had left her husband—to marry someone in Italy almost twenty years younger than she was.
Patty had tremendous sympathy for Angelina regarding
this. But she wanted to say right now: Listen to this! Lucy
Barton's mother was awful to her, and her father—oh dear

God, her father . . . But Lucy *loved* them, she loved her mother, and her mother loved her! We're all just a mess, Angelina, trying as hard as we can, we love *imperfectly*, Angelina, but it's okay.

Patty had been dying to tell her friend this, but she sensed now how paltry—almost nutty—her words would seem. And so Patty listened about Angelina's children, in high school, almost ready to fly the coop, she listened about the mother in Italy, how she emailed all her girls—Angelina had four sisters—and how Angelina was the only one who had not gone to see her mother, but Angelina was thinking about it, she might go this summer.

"Oh, go," said Patty. "Do go. I think you should. I mean, she's *old*, Angelina."

"I know."

Patty was aware of how much Angelina wanted to talk about herself, and yet this didn't disturb Patty, she merely noticed it. And she understood. Everyone, she understood, was mainly and mostly interested in themselves. Except Sibby had been interested in her, and she had been terribly interested in him. This was the skin that protected you from the world—this loving of another person you shared your life with.

A while later, well into her second glass of white wine, Patty told Angelina about Lila Lane, but she said only the Fatty Patty stuff, and how they all thought she was a virgin. And then she said, "You know, Lucy Barton wrote—"

"Oh, for the love of God," said Angelina. "You're as pretty as ever, Patty. Honest to God, to have to listen to that. No one calls you that, Patty."

"They might."

"I've never heard it, and I hear kids all day long. Patty, you can still meet a man. You're lovely. You really are."

"Charlie Macauley is the only man who interests me," Patty said. This was the wine.

"He's old, Patty! You know, he's a mess."

"In what way is he a mess?"

"I just mean he was in the Vietnam war years ago and he's— You know, he's got terrible PTSD."

"He does?"

Angelina gave a tiny shrug. "I heard that. I don't know who from. But years ago I heard it. I don't know, really. His wife is— Well, you've got a chance, Patty."

Patty laughed. "His wife always seemed nice."

"Oh, come on, she's an anxious old thing. I'm telling you, go for a spin with Charlie."

And then Patty wished she hadn't said anything.

But Angelina didn't seem to notice. It was herself—and her husband—she wanted to talk about. "I asked him right out the other night on the phone, are you going to start divorce proceedings, and he said no, he didn't want to do that. So I let it drop. I don't know why he'd leave but not want a divorce. Oh, Patty!"

In the parking lot, Angelina put her arms around Patty

and they hugged, squeezed each other tight, for a moment. "I love you," Angelina called out as she got into her car, and Patty said, "Back at you."

Patty drove carefully. The wine had made her feel things, although she was not supposed to drink with her anti-depressants. But her mind felt large now, and through it went many things. She thought of Sebastian, and wondered if anyone knew what she had not known until he told her— the unspeakable things that had happened to him. She wondered now if it had showed. Something showed, certainly. She remembered how she'd heard in the clothing store one day, as she'd left with Sebastian, the young clerk saying to another clerk, "It's like she has a dog."

In Lucy Barton's memoir, Lucy wrote how people were always looking to feel superior to someone else, and Patty thought this was true.

Tonight the moon was behind Patty, almost, and she saw it in the rearview mirror and winked at it. Her sister Linda came into her mind. Linda saying she didn't know how Patty could work with adolescents. Patty, driving, shook her head; well, that's because Linda never knew. No one except Sebastian ever knew. After Sibby's death, Patty had gone to a therapist. She had planned on telling this woman. But the woman wore a navy blue blazer and sat behind a big desk, and she asked Patty how she felt about her parents' divorce. Bad, Patty had said. Patty couldn't figure out how to stop going to this therapist, until she lied and said she couldn't afford it anymore.

Now, as Patty drove into her driveway and saw the lights she'd left on, she realized that Lucy Barton's book had understood her. That was it—the book had understood her. There remained that sweetness of a yellow-colored candy in her mouth. Lucy Barton had her own shame; oh boy did she have her own shame. And she had risen right straight out of it. "Huh," said Patty, as she turned the car engine off. She sat in the car for a few moments before she finally got out and went inside.

✳

On Monday morning Patty left a note with the homeroom teacher asking Lila Lane to come to her office, but she was surprised nevertheless when the girl showed up the next period. "Lila," said Patty. "Come in."

The girl walked into Patty's office, and Patty said, "Have a seat." The girl looked at her warily, but she spoke right away and said, "I bet you want me to apologize."

"No," Patty said. "Nope. I asked you to come here today because the last time you were here I called you a piece of filth."

The girl looked confused.

Patty said, "When you were in here last week, I called you a piece of filth."

"You did?" the girl asked. She sat down slowly.

"I did."

"I don't remember." The girl was not belligerent.

"After you asked why I had no children and said I was a virgin and called me Fatty Patty, I called you a piece of filth."

The girl watched her with suspicion.

"You are not a piece of filth." Patty waited, and the girl waited, and then Patty said, "When I was growing up in Hanston, my father was a manager of a feed corn farm and we had plenty of money. We were comfortable, you'd call it. We had enough money. I have no business calling you—calling anyone—a piece of filth."

The girl shrugged. "I am."

"No, you're *not*."

"Well, I guess you were angry."

"Of course I was angry. You were really rude to me. But that did not give me the right to say what I said."

The girl seemed tired; she had circles under her eyes. "I wouldn't worry about it," she said. "I wouldn't think about it anymore if I were you."

"Listen," Patty said. "You have very good scores and excellent grades. You could go to school if you wanted to. Do you want to?"

The girl looked vaguely surprised. She shrugged. "I dunno."

"My husband," Patty said, "thought he was filth."

The girl looked at her. After a moment she said, "He did?"

"He did. Because of things that had happened to him."

The girl looked at Patty with large, sad-looking eyes. She finally let out a long sigh. "Oh boy," she said. "Well. I'm sorry I said that shit about you. That stuff about you."

Patty said, "You're sixteen."

"Fifteen."

"You're fifteen. I'm the adult, and I'm the one who did something wrong."

Patty was startled to see that tears had begun to slip down the girl's face, and the girl wiped them with her hand. "I'm just tired," Lila said. "I'm just so tired."

Patty got up and closed the door to her office. "Sweetie," she said. "Listen to me, honey. I can do something for you. I can get you into a school. There will be money somewhere. Your grades are excellent, like I said. I was surprised to see your grades, and your scores are really high. My grades weren't as good as yours are, and I went to school because my parents could afford to send me. But I can get you into a school, and you can go."

The girl put her head down on her arms on Patty's desk. Her shoulders shook. In a few minutes she said, looking up, her face wet, "I'm sorry. But when someone's nice to me— Oh God, it just kills me."

"That's okay," Patty said.

"No, it's not." The girl wept again, steadily and with noise. "Oh God," she said, wiping at her face.

Patty handed her a tissue. "It's okay. I'm telling you. It is all going to be okay."

⁎

The sun was bright, washing over the steps of the post office as Patty walked up them that afternoon. In the post office was Charlie Macauley. "Hi, Patty," he said, and nodded.

"Charlie Macauley," she said. "I'm seeing you everywhere these days. How are you?"

"Surviving." He was headed for the door.

She checked her mailbox, pulled from it the mail, and was aware that he had left. But when she walked outside he was sitting on the steps, and to her surprise—only it was not that surprising—she sat down next to him. "Whoa," she said, "I may not be able to get up again." The step was cement, and she felt the chill of it through her pants, though the sun shone down.

Charlie shrugged. "So don't. Let's just sit."

Later, for years to come, Patty would go over it in her mind, their sitting on the steps, how it seemed outside of time. Across the street was the hardware store, and beyond that was a blue house, the side of it lit with the afternoon sun. It was the tall white windmills that came to her mind. How their skinny long arms all turned, but never together, except for just once in a while two of them would be turning in unison, their arms poised at the same place in the sky.

Eventually Charlie said, "You doing okay these days, Patty?"

She said, "I am, I'm fine," and turned to look at him. His eyes seemed to go back forever, they were that deep.

After a few moments Charlie said, "You're a Midwestern girl, so you say things are fine. But they may not always be fine."

She said nothing, watching him. She saw how right above his Adam's apple he had forgotten to shave; a few white whiskers were there.

"You sure don't have to tell me what's not fine," he said, looking straight ahead now, "and I'm sure not going to ask. I'm just here to say that sometimes"—and he turned his eyes back to hers, his eyes were pale blue, she noticed— "that sometimes things aren't so fine, no siree bob. They aren't always fine."

Oh, she wanted to say, wanting to put her hand on his. Because it was himself he was speaking of, this came to her then. Oh, Charlie, she wanted to say. But she sat next to him quietly, and a car went by on Main Street, then another. "Lucy Barton wrote a memoir," Patty finally said.

"Lucy Barton." Charlie stared straight ahead, squinted. "The Barton kids, Jesus, that poor boy, the oldest kid." He shook his head just slightly. "Jesus Christ. Poor kids. Jesus H. Christ." He looked at Patty. "I suppose it's a sad book?"

"It's not. At least I didn't think so." Patty thought about this. She said, "It made me feel better, it made me feel much less alone."

Charlie shook his head. "Oh no. No, we're always alone." For quite a while they sat in companionable silence with the sun beating down on them. Then Patty said, "We're not *always* alone."

Charlie turned to look at her. He said nothing.

"Can I ask you?" Patty said. "Did people think my husband was strange?"

Charlie waited a moment, as though considering this. "Maybe. I'm the last person around here to know what people think. Sebastian seemed to me to be a good man. In pain. He was in pain."

"Yuh. He was." Patty nodded.

Charlie said, "I'm sorry about that."

"I know you are." The sun splashed brightly against the blue house.

After many moments had gone by, Charlie turned again to look at her. He opened his mouth as though about to say something, but then he shook his head and closed his mouth once more. Patty felt—without knowing what it was—that she understood what he was going to say.

She touched his arm just briefly, and in the sun they sat.

Cracked

When Linda Peterson-Cornell saw the woman who would be staying in their home for the week, she thought: Oh, this will be the one. The woman's name was Yvonne Tuttle, and she had been brought to the house by another woman from the photography festival, Karen-Lucie Toth, who stood silently beside Yvonne as Linda welcomed her. Yvonne was very tall and had slightly wavy brown hair that went to her shoulders; her face had possibly been quite pretty ten years earlier. Now there were lines beneath the eyes that diminished their blue gaze, and also Yvonne wore too much makeup for someone who was clearly past forty—Linda was fifty-five. Yvonne's sandals, with high cork wedges, made her even taller. They gave away to Linda the fact that Yvonne had, in her youth, most likely not come from much. Shoes always gave you away.

In the garden of Linda and Jay Peterson-Cornell's house

were two sculptures by Alexander Calder, both on one side of the large and bright blue swimming pool; inside the house on the walls of the living room were two Picassos and an Edward Hopper. There was also an early Philip Guston at the end of the sloping hallway that led to the guest area.

"Come," Linda directed, and both the other women followed her down the hallway, which swerved around a corner then led through the long, glass-paneled walkway that finally opened into the guest suite. Linda nodded to the maid to indicate that she could leave, then Linda waited for Yvonne to say something. Yvonne just kept glancing around, gripping the handle of her wheelie suitcase, and said nothing about the house, which, even if you did not recognize the art on the walls—astonishing for a photographer not to recognize art—was still worth commenting on. The house had been renovated a few years earlier, and what the architect had done was inspired. The guestroom was all glass.

"Where's the door?" Yvonne finally said.

"There is no door," Linda said. She could have told Yvonne that there was no need to worry about privacy, as she and her husband stayed upstairs in the front of the house and the back garden had no houses overlooking it, but Linda did not say this. Instead she showed Yvonne the bathroom across the hall, which also had no door and was in the shape of a V and had no shower curtain or stall, the shower nozzle simply protruded from the wall. The floor was tilted to take the running water away.

CRACKED   65

"I've never seen anything like this," Yvonne said, and Linda told her that everyone said that. Karen-Lucie Toth had continued to stand silently near Yvonne this whole time: She was the most famous of the photographers at the Summer Festival and the one who came back every year. Linda knew that Karen-Lucie had asked if Yvonne Tuttle could teach a class this summer, and the directors had agreed, although Yvonne's portfolio was not as strong as the Festival usually required. But no one at the Festival wanted to lose Karen-Lucie: The students loved her, and her work was well-known, and also Karen-Lucie's husband had thrown himself off the top of the Sheraton in Fort Lauderdale three years before. Karen-Lucie Toth got a pass on everything, including politeness, Linda thought, because when she said now to Karen-Lucie, "I don't believe you've been inside this house before," Karen-Lucie, also tall, also with brown hair—they could have been sisters, Linda observed—only said, in her extraordinarily thick Alabama accent, "I have not."

After that, Yvonne and Karen-Lucie went away, and Linda, watching through the kitchen window as they walked down the road, saw them talking intently to each other and felt sure they were talking about her. Linda was jealous of Karen-Lucie Toth—she knew this, it was not a suppressed feeling—because Karen-Lucie was famous and childless and still pretty, and because she had no husband. Linda would have liked her own husband, whose intelligence had once impressed her so, to simply disappear.

✳

The town hosting the photography festival was a small town about an hour outside of Chicago, with a library and a school and a church and a bright red hardware store that had a row of mason jars in its front window. There were also two cafés and three restaurants and one bar that at night often played live music. The houses near the center of town were large and old and well-kept, their porches cluttered this time of year with big pots of geraniums and petunias. The trees in town were tall oaks and black walnuts, and the boughs of honey locusts and chokecherries were pendulous, so that when there were no children playing in the park or in the schoolyard the trees could be heard with their own sound of whispers, and sometimes there was the tinkling sound of ash leaves too. A private high school that had gone bankrupt years earlier and eventually been forced to close was still available—parts of it—for the classrooms of the photography festival. In order to get to these buildings you needed to walk through pathways so thick with bushes and tree boughs that houses were only glimpsed as one passed by. It had almost a fairy-tale quality to it, the town. Yvonne Tuttle said this to Karen-Lucie Toth, and Karen-Lucie said she thought that too. They had just arrived at the building where a welcoming reception was being held.

Joy Gunterson, the director of the festival, had black

ringlets and she was short and strikingly skinny. She thanked Yvonne for coming, saying that she was happy to include any friend of Karen-Lucie Toth's. It seemed to Yvonne that Joy Gunterson's eyes kept looking up toward the ceiling during this conversation, and after Joy walked away Yvonne told this to Karen-Lucie, who said "Oh, remind me" just as a woman walked up to them, dressed like someone from the sixties, with a pillbox hat, and a short coat, and a little pocketbook that matched her high heels; this woman threw her arms around Karen-Lucie, and Yvonne saw that the woman was a man. "I'm crazy about Karen-Lucie," he told Yvonne, and Karen-Lucie puckered her lips and said, "Dollface, yew are just the *sweetest* little boyfriend I know."

"You two look like sisters," the man said. His shaved beard showed through his makeup, and his features were fine, almost perfect in their proportions.

"We are sisters," Yvonne answered. "Ripped apart at birth."

"Savagely," Karen-Lucie added. "But we're together now. Look at that sweet pocketbook on your darlin' wrist."

"What's your name?" Yvonne asked.

"Tomasina. Here. At home, Tom." He gave a graceful shrug, a subdued girlish bounce.

"Got it," Yvonne said.

※

Linda did not comment as she got into bed next to her husband, and Jay did not comment either, although it was unusual these days for Linda to watch with him. On the laptop that Jay held against his knees they both gazed at Yvonne, who had arrived back at the house so late that neither of them had stayed in the living room waiting for her. Now she tossed her keys onto the bed, and her sigh could be heard through the audio. Yvonne put her hands to her hips and looked all around her. Then she went into the bathroom, where the cameras caught her staring so intently at the shower nozzle, which naturally gave the effect of Yvonne staring straight at them, that a shot of fear went through Linda, but Yvonne—surprising to Linda—chose not to shower and only used the toilet instead, washed her face, brushed her teeth, and came back into the guestroom, where she stood again, looking through the huge panes of glass that now showed the blackness of night. Finally she opened her small suitcase and undressed. Her body was more youthful-looking than Linda would have thought, but height could do that for you. Her breasts were still firm-appearing, and her thighs were—in the somewhat grainy light of the camera—smooth. She kept her underpants on and donned a pair of white pajamas that gave her the look, with her hair now in a low ponytail, of someone almost as young as their daughter. But of course she was not; she was a middle-aged woman a long way from her home in Arizona, and she reached for her cellphone and the ringing sounded quietly through the laptop on Jay's knees.

"Talk low," they heard Yvonne say. "I've got you on speakerphone while I unpack. I mean, this guest house, or room, or whatever it is, is miles away, but you never know. Jeeze."

"Hey, honey child." Unmistakably the voice of Karen-Lucie Toth. "You okay?"

"No," said Yvonne. Her voice was muffled; she was facing away, pulling things from her suitcase. "It's creepy here, Karen-Lucie. How'm I ever going to sleep?"

"Take a pill, honey. You know, I think I heard they got all their money from his father, who was in plastics. What's that mean, I wonder, to be in plastics? The weirdos you're staying with. They're in plastics. Can you take a pill, baby doll?"

"Yeah, I will." As Yvonne spoke, she sat on the bed and rummaged through her bag, and Linda and Jay watched her squint at a pill bottle, which she opened. Then she brought from the same bag two small bottles of wine, the type that could be purchased on an airplane. She unscrewed the top from one and tilted it back. "I know you're tired," she said. "I'm really okay." She added, "That Tom, or Tomasina, his wife doesn't mind?"

"Not as long as he does it away from home and without the kids around."

"I'd mind."

Karen-Lucie said, "But if you really loved him—"

"Maybe I wouldn't mind, I don't know. I honestly don't know. Good night. I love you."

"Love you too, baby."

Linda glanced at her husband's profile. She said, "She didn't even shower, and she traveled all day."

Jay put a finger to his lips and nodded. Linda rose then and left the room to sleep across the hall, as she always did. Ever since her daughter moved away, saying those awful things about her, Linda had slept away from her husband.

※

Seven years earlier a young woman in town had disappeared. She was a sophomore in high school and a cheerleader and also she babysat for the families of the Episcopalian church of which her family was a member. So there were many people to investigate and of course the town was in dreadful distress. A deep resentment of the media—which swarmed the town with an almost biblical descent of cameras and large furry microphones and trucks with huge satellite dishes that scooped at the air—the resentment of this united most people, but then strange alliances formed and ruptured according to what theory was popular that day, for example, when the Driver's Ed teacher was thought to be a suspect—that really divided people. And then there were a few who said the girl had actually run away, that nobody knew the terrible things that took place in her home, and this added to the dismay and horror that her poor parents and siblings endured. For two years the town lived this way.

During this time Linda Peterson-Cornell existed with a confusing disc of darkness deep inside her chest, and as she watched her husband read the news reports, and follow the case on TV, she often broke out in a sweat. She thought she had to be crazy. She could not imagine why her body was reacting this way, why her mind itself could not stay calm. And then when it was over, finally, finally over, she forgot that she had felt this way. Only occasionally would she remember, but never with the visceral aspect of what she had actually gone through. And each time she remembered she thought: I'm a silly woman, I have *nothing* to complain about, not really, not like that, Jesus God.

The second night of the festival Linda sat reading in the living room with her husband, and Yvonne came through the front door and walked past them down the ramp to the lower floor. She flapped a hand as she went by. "G'night," she called.

"But how are you?" Jay called back. "How's the teaching going?"

"Fine!" This was said from downstairs. "Got an early class. Good *night*," she called again. They could hear the very faint sound of the shower—not long—and they sat reading in the living room for another two hours.

In the middle of the night—through the shield of her sleeping pill—Linda was aware of her husband in the shower. It was not unusual, particularly, but it gave Linda a sense of unease; it always did, and tonight reminded her of what she had felt seven years before. Just the relief of that time now being over allowed her to fall back into sleep.

✳

Each night Karen-Lucie and Yvonne went to the bar that played live music. Each night they asked Tomasina if he wanted to go with them, and each night Tomasina said no, he was going back to his room to call his wife and his kids and to read over the assignments for the next day. "He's not a bad photographer," Karen-Lucie told Yvonne. "If he loved it with his whole heart he might be really good. But he doesn't love it with his whole heart. He just comes here be- cause . . ."

They nodded simultaneously, picking at the corn chips in the basket on the table. "Bless his soul," Karen-Lucie added.

"Totally. And his wife's too."

"Hell yeah." Karen-Lucie put a hand to her mouth. "Yvie, I was betrayed. *Bee*-trayed. I want you to know that."

Yvonne nodded.

"That's all I'm going to say."

Yvonne nodded again.

"My heart is broken," Karen-Lucie said.

"I know that," Yvonne said.

"Broken. He broke my heart." Karen-Lucie flicked a corn chip and it flew across the table.

After a number of minutes went by, Yvonne asked, "Why do Joy's eyes roll around when she's talking to me?"

"Oh. 'Cause her son killed a girl here years ago and buried her in the backyard and then finally told his mama. Yes, darlin', I am serious." Karen-Lucie nodded. "He's in prison now for the rest of his life, however long or short that may be. Joy and her husband got divorced and her husband got all the money—they were rich but he got all the money—and Joy lives in a trailer now, outside of town, and if you go there you will see a photograph she has on her mantel, taken of her standing right next to her son, and she has her hand on his chest in this gesture of affection, but it covers up the numbers on his uniform so the photograph looks like he's just wearing a dark blue shirt."

"God," Yvonne said. "My *God*."

"I know."

"How old was he when he did this?"

"Fifteen, I think. Sixteen? They charged him as an adult because he didn't tell anyone for almost two years. Just left her buried in their backyard. If he'd told, he wouldn't have gotten life. But he got life. Without parole."

"A dog didn't dig up the body?"

"No, ma'am, that did not happen. I guess he buried her deep enough." Karen-Lucie held up two fingers. "Two years, and he says, Mama—I got to tell you something."

"What happened to the family of the girl?"

"They moved. Joy's ex-husband left too. Won't have

anything to do with his son at all. Wiped his hands clean. Joy goes every month to see her boy in Joliet."

Yvonne shook her head slowly, drew her fingers through her hair. "Whew," she said.

After a long silence, Karen-Lucie said, "I'm awful sorry you never had your kids, Yvie, I know you wanted kids so bad."

"Well," said Yvonne. "You know."

"You'd have been a good mama, I do know that."

Yvonne looked at her friend. "It's life. It's all just friggin' life."

"Yes, it is," Karen-Lucie said. "Yes, it is."

✳

The next morning, which was three mornings after she had first arrived, Yvonne Tuttle approached Linda at the kitchen sink. Linda had not known Yvonne was still in the house and she was startled to find the woman standing behind her as she washed her coffee cup. "Have you seen my white pajamas?" Yvonne asked with direct curiosity.

"Why would I have seen your pajamas?" Linda placed the coffee cup in the drainer.

"Well, because they're missing. I mean, they're just *gone*. And things don't just go. If you see what I mean."

"I don't." Linda dried her hands on the dish towel.

"Well, I mean my white pajamas that I put each morning beneath my pillow are gone." Yvonne made a sign with her arms, like an umpire calling it safe. "Gone. And they have to be somewhere, so I thought I'd ask. I mean, maybe the maid took them to wash them or something."

"The maid did not take your white pajamas."

Yvonne looked at her for a long moment. "Huh," she said.

Linda felt fury rising in her, almost uncontrollable. "We do not go stealing things in this house."

"I was just asking," Yvonne said.

✳

During the last weekend of the festival a show was mounted in the same room at the former private high school where the welcoming reception had been. On one side were the faculty photographs, and on the other were student photographs. Yvonne stood with Karen-Lucie and Tomasina off to the side, watching people move slowly around the room. "I hate this," Yvonne said.

Tomasina switched his pocketbook to his other wrist. "Karen-Lucie, do you get used to people staring at your photographs? Look at the way that woman there is tilting her head, she's *wondering*. Wondering what the cracked plates in your photos mean."

Karen-Lucie said, "They mean I'm cracked up."

Tomasina smiled with deep affection at Karen-Lucie. "You crack *me* up," he said.

"Sweetheart, I wanna take you home. You know, that lady's a rich culture vulture, I can just tell by the back of her head. Shittin' in high cotton, that girl. Just buy the damn thing." Karen-Lucie turned away.

"Oh God, she's the woman whose house I'm in," said Yvonne. "Oh, let's go."

Karen-Lucie said, "Right now, baby doll."

The sun was very bright and they all three stood for a moment on the wooden porch, squinting. Tomasina reached for his sunglasses. "It's hot," he said. "I didn't know it was so hot outside. I have my nylons on."

"They look nice," Yvonne said. "You look nice."

"Doesn't he always just look so nice?" Karen-Lucie made a kissing sound in Tomasina's direction. "Lord, it is hotter than two rabbits screwin' in a wool sock."

A man's voice startled them from behind. "Girls and boys," it said. It was Jay Peterson-Cornell. He had just stepped through the door they had walked through. "Had enough of your exhibit?" he asked. He held out his hand toward Karen-Lucie. "I'm Jay," he said, and for a moment the sunlight glinted on his glasses, then his eyes came into view. "A real pleasure to meet you. Love your work."

"Thank you," Karen-Lucie said.

"Can I get you girls something cool to drink?"

Karen-Lucie said, "We have an appointment, I'm afraid."

"I see." Jay turned in the direction of Yvonne. "We haven't seen much of you this week. Have you enjoyed yourself in our little town? Or do you find it dull compared to the funky scene of Tucson?"

"I like your little town." Yvonne felt sweat run down her back.

"Come on, y'all. Nice to meet you, Mr. Jay." Karen-Lucie moved to the steps, and Yvonne and Tomasina followed. The three of them walked single file through the pathway in the woods that led back toward town, and none of them spoke until they came to a clearing by the church.

"I need a drink," said Yvonne.

In the bar, Tomasina said, "He didn't even acknowledge me, did you notice?"

"'Course not, honey," said Karen-Lucie. "He ain't gonna acknowledge anyone he can't *do*."

"I don't know why he makes me feel creepy," said Yvonne.

"Because he is creepy. I'm telling you." Karen-Lucie pointed her swizzle stick at Yvonne.

"It's not like he looks creepy. He looks normal." Yvonne picked up a chip, put it back into the basket.

Karen-Lucie let out a long sigh. "For a hundred years I waitressed in my youth, and, child, I got to know some things. I got to know men's eyes." Karen-Lucie tapped the swizzle stick to her cheekbone. "And *this* man, baby doll, thinks *yew* are a big old tall piece of trash, that's what he thinks. He'd think the same about me, but I've won some a-wards, and he'd rather hang me on his wall. And when you win your a-wards, and you will, Yvie, he'll want you on his wall beside his fuckin' freezing cold Pee-casso. But right now he is sniffin' your panties and tuckin' your pretty white pajamas under his pillow each night."

Yvonne gave small nods. "Thank you." She added, "I'm serious."

"I know you're serious."

"Whoa," said Tomasina. "This is sad stuff I'm hearing."

Karen-Lucie looked at Tomasina's profile with a serious hard look. Then she put her hand on his and said, "You are to worry about nothing. You are doing just fine."

✳

Linda and Jay Peterson-Cornell sat in the living room waiting up to speak to their houseguest. Every night she had come in later and later, and when she came in she always said "Hello, g'night" and kept right on walking down the ramp in her wedge-heeled sandals.

The night after Jay and Linda had been to the exhibit, Jay said, "She doesn't give us the time of day."

Without looking at him, turning the page of her magazine, Linda said, "When I first saw her I thought maybe you'd run off with her."

Jay laughed. "Did you? Because of her slightly slutty, kind of working-class look?"

"I don't think it's just a look," Linda said.

"No. Clearly not."

Linda should have sensed—she did sense—her husband's heightened state. She did not watch with him again
the view of Yvonne in the bedroom or the bathroom. She
did not mention to him that Yvonne had reported her white
pajamas missing. On the last night of Yvonne's stay, Linda
sat with him in the living room, and toward midnight
Yvonne came in. "You've been burning your candle at both
ends," Jay called out to her.

"I have been. Sleep well," Yvonne called back, disap-
pearing down the ramp.

"Would you come here for a moment, please?" Jay
called. He stayed sitting and Linda sat next to him, holding
a newspaper open on her lap.

After a moment, Yvonne came back up the ramp. "Yes?"
she said.

"Have you a family?" Jay asked her. "Are you divorced?"

"Am I divorced?"

"That's what I asked."

"Well. *Jeeze.*" Yvonne put a hand to her forehead.
"There's a conversation starter. Is that the first thing you
usually ask middle-aged women when you meet them?"

"You look divorced," Jay said.

Yvonne shook her head quickly in tiny gestures. "Okay.
If you'll excuse me, I'm going to bed."

"You've stayed in our house for more than a week,"
Linda said. "And you've never once had a conversation with
us. You'll understand if we feel—rebuffed. We opened our
home to you."

"Oh. Okay. Yeah, I'm sorry." This seemed to have hit home, and Linda sensed immediately how little confidence the woman really had. How her mother had probably tried to bring her up right but a desperation was inherited. Yvonne stepped into the living room. "I didn't mean to be rude. I've just been really tired each night."

"Sit," Jay said pleasantly, nodding toward a chair.

The woman sat. Her legs were very long and the chair she sat in was low to the ground, so her knees stuck up like a cricket's. Linda could see she was uncomfortable, and Linda was not sorry.

"So tell us. You live in Arizona? Have you lived there long?" Linda asked.

"Yeah," said Yvonne. "Basically. You know, most of my adult life."

"Our daughter was thinking of moving to New Mexico, but she went east instead," Jay said, smiling. "She lives in Boston now."

"Yeah? How old is she?"

"She's twenty-three and very much enjoying her independence from us. It's natural at that age." Jay was still smiling. "She has a twin brother who lives in Providence, and he's enjoying his independence as well," he added.

"Karen-Lucie has done some wonderful work recently," Linda said.

"Hasn't she?" Yvonne sat forward, but her knees were too high so she had to sit back and stretch her legs out and she looked undeniably inviting. "The whole earthquake series. I think she's brilliant. Those cracked plates." Yvonne shook her head appreciatively, tried sitting up straight again.

"Some artists are so competitive. Even with their friends," Jay said. "But I guess you can be generous since your own work's been successful. And rightly so, might I add."

"I'm sure you're just generous anyway," Linda said. She thought Yvonne looked wary. "Let me get us some wine," she said. There was no doubt about what she felt. Jay had had his successes before, but Linda had never felt as complicit.

In another twenty minutes Linda excused herself and went to bed.

She listened intently, and fairly soon she heard Yvonne going downstairs and walking through the walkway to her room. The door to her husband's room shut quietly, and Linda took her sleeping pill.

Somewhere in a dream Linda heard screaming; the sound was terrifying. "Honey," said Jay. He was speaking to her from the doorway and her bedroom light was on. "There's been a little issue."

Sitting up quickly, she was certain she heard the doorbell ring. She said, "Jay, I was just dreaming—"

"Let me do the talking," Jay said. He smiled at her, but she thought he looked different, as though his face was broader than she had noticed before, and his face was moist with perspiration. She put on her robe and followed him downstairs. When he opened the door, two policemen stood there. Linda saw behind them another policeman and also a policewoman and, in the driveway, the two white police cars. The policemen were very polite. "Can you show us where the guestroom is? Where you had the guest Yvonne Tuttle staying?"

Jay said, "Of course. Linda, take them down."

Linda's mouth was extremely dry as she turned to go down the ramp to the guest area. The bedroom was in darkness, and as Linda started to enter, her hand reaching for the light switch, the policewoman stopped her, saying, "No, please leave everything." And the policeman said, "Mrs. Peterson, why don't you go back upstairs now?"

Linda turned quickly, calling out for Jay.

Jay was shaking his head slowly as the policemen stood in the kitchen with their arms at their sides. "We thought she seemed odd from the very beginning, but I'm sure you understand I don't care to discuss any more of this without speaking to my lawyer. I'm represented by Norm Atwood, and you know what he'll say. This is outlandish, entirely ridiculous. I don't imagine the county looks forward to a lawsuit from me."

One of the policemen said, "Why don't you ask him to meet us at the station?"

"Honestly." Jay smiled. "I know you folks pride yourselves on being meticulous, but this is *just* outrageous."

"Where's Yvonne?" Linda suddenly asked, as the men were gathering by the door.

"She's at the county hospital, ma'am," said one of the policemen.

"She says I tried to rape her," Jay added.

"Yvonne? She *did*? But that's *insane*," Linda said.

"Of course it's insane," Jay said calmly. "Honey, I'll be back soon."

The policewoman stayed behind with one of the policemen. Linda said, "What are you doing?"

"Have a seat, Mrs. Peterson. We'd like to ask you a few questions." They were very polite. They asked about Yvonne. What was she like?

"Oh, horrible!" Linda said.

In what way?

"She was rude to us, never spending time with us." Linda suddenly remembered about the pajamas and blurted that out too. "She accused me of—of stealing her pajamas." The policewoman nodded sympathetically while the policeman wrote something down.

"And was she rude to your husband as well?"

Too late, Linda realized that she should have said nothing. They were very nice to her when she said she was not going to talk to them anymore. They explained that a search warrant was being obtained for the guestroom, that evidence might be taken, possibly the sheets, pillowcases, things like that.

*

The next morning, Jay slept heavily in their bedroom. Toward dawn, Norm Atwood had brought him home. Jay had been charged with third-degree battery and released on bond. Norm explained that Jay had most likely been charged because Yvonne was in such a condition of hysteria, running down the road at three A.M. in underpants and a T-shirt, then knocking on a door in town, and that there was a small bruise on her wrist that could conceivably indicate a struggle. Norm said the state would still have difficulty proving it was not an encounter of consent, that it was always hard to prove, with no witnesses, the matter of consent. Now Linda sat motionless in the back garden beside the glaring blue swimming pool. In her pocket her cellphone rang, and she clicked it on.

Her daughter said, "Fuck you, Mom. Just fuck you both. I'm never coming home again."

Linda rose and went inside to the living room and sat on the far end of the couch. She felt a little bit out-of-body because she had a sensation of being young again, walking down a road on an early summer evening with school girl friends past fields and fields of corn and fields of soybeans, the whole world filled with the bright green of new life, the sun setting so that the entire sky was colored in glorious celebration, the air on her bare arms she recalled too, all freedom, all innocence, the laughter—

Norm Atwood had arranged an appointment for her in

the afternoon to drive to Layton to see her own lawyer: She
had marital privilege, he explained—she didn't have to testify against Jay about anything he had told her. But anything she had seen she would be put on the stand to report
under oath. Linda tried to understand this as she sat on the
couch, but she felt that all parts of her had stopped; she
was in neutral. She looked about her. The Hopper painting
hung on the wall with an indifference so vast it began to feel
personal, as though it had been painted for this moment:
Your troubles are huge and meaningless, it seemed to say,
there is only the sun on the side of a house. She got up and
moved into the dining room, sitting at the long table. A few
years earlier, her daughter had found something on her father's computer, and the girl had screamed and screamed
and screamed. Dad screws women right in the house, and
you do *nothing*? You're more pathetic than he is, Mom, you
make me *sick*.

It had started as a private game, a way of breaking domestic boredom, creating a Linda Peterson-Cornell that
seemed daring, provocative, a person her husband appreci-
ated more.

※

While Linda was growing up in northern Illinois, her father
had managed a successful feed corn farm. Her mother, a
homemaker, had been a scattered woman, but kind; their
last name was Nicely, and Linda and her two sisters were

known as the Pretty Nicely Girls. It was a pleasant childhood, and then her mother suddenly, so suddenly it seemed
to Linda to happen while she was at school one day, moved
out and into a squalid little apartment, and it was the most
terrible thing Linda could imagine, worse than if her
mother had died. After a few months her mother wanted to
return home, but Linda's father refused to allow it, and the
image of her mother living alone in a tiny house—after the
squalid apartment—and having given up her friends, all of
whom reacted with fear as though her mother's attempts at
freedom might be contagious, terminal, along with the es-
trangement of her daughters, because their father pulled
their loyalty to him; all this was—by far—the strongest
event in Linda's life. The week after Linda graduated from
high school she married a local boy named Bill Peterson,
then she divorced him one year later, keeping his name. In
college in Wisconsin she met Jay, who with his intelligence
and vast money seemed to offer a life that might catapult
her away from the terrifying and abiding image of her
mother alone and ostracized.

Now, as Linda sat at the end of the dining room table, the
doorbell rang, though at first she wasn't sure she had heard
right. It rang again. She peeked through the curtains and
did not see anyone, so she opened the door cautiously and
it was skinny Joy Gunterson, saying, "Linda, I just had to
come over."

Linda said, "No you didn't, no you did not. You have nothing in common with me, do you hear? You have nothing in common with me. Go away."

"Oh, Linda. But I *do*—"

"I'm not going to end up living in some trailer, Joy." It amazed her that she said this, no part of her had any inkling she would say that. It seemed to amaze Joy too. The woman, shorter than Linda, had a look of confusion shift onto her face.

Probably this mutual surprise prevented Linda from closing the door. So Joy had time to shake her head and say, "Oh, but, Linda—see, it doesn't matter where you live. That's what you find out. When the person you love more than anyone spends his days in a cell, then you're in a cell too. It doesn't matter where you are. You'll find out who're your real friends. They won't be who you think. Trust me on that."

Linda closed the door and locked it.

She went to the door of Jay's bedroom, but he was still fast asleep and snoring, lying flat on his back. Without glasses his face seemed naked; she had not seen him sleeping for some time. She closed the door and went back downstairs. She did not know what she would say to this lawyer. Norm had said it also depended on whether or not Yvonne continued to want to press charges. A lot depended on Yvonne.

Linda walked around the house quietly. She understood that her mind was trying to take in something it could not

take in. She thought of Karen-Lucie Toth, who must be
with Yvonne right now; the police had come to collect
Yvonne's things and return them to her. Linda had not
asked where Yvonne was. In the kitchen sink were two white
mugs with coffee stains; Linda couldn't say who had been
drinking coffee, how they'd got into the sink. As she washed
them, her legs almost gave way. She pictured jurors sitting
in a jury box. She pictured Yvonne, with her too much
makeup, on the stand. And then she thought of the cameras; why in the world had she not thought of the cameras?
*Did you, or did you not, watch women with your husband
while they undressed, showered, used the toilet? How long
had you been aware that your husband was watching them
this way?*

✳

Driving toward Layton, Linda stopped at a gas station a
few miles outside of town. She felt horribly exposed and so
did not pull in to the self-serve dock, but instead had a man
fill up her tank. But then she suddenly had to use the bathroom. With her sunglasses on she went into the store, past
the rows of cellophane-wrapped doughnuts and cakes and
peanuts and candy. The filth of the bathroom appalled her.
She could not remember the last time she had used a public
restroom this filthy, and she thought: Why should it matter
when now nothing matters? Her mind was scrambled like

that, so when she walked back through the store and bumped straight into Karen-Lucie Toth they stared at each other with amazement. Karen-Lucie was also wearing sunglasses; she removed them, and her eyes, to Linda, seemed older than Linda would have thought, and sad, and still pretty.

"You scared me," Linda said.

"Well. You scared me too."

They moved together down the aisle away from the foot traffic. Tall Karen-Lucie spoke down. "Ma'am, as God's truth, after my own tragedy a few years back, I feel sometimes that I have compassion for everyone. I do. It's probably the only blessing that came from that. But your husband scared my friend, he scared her *bad*."

"Where is she?"

"I just took her to the airport. She needs to get home and see a proper doctor."

"Listen," Linda said. "I have no idea about any of it."

Karen-Lucie's pretty eyes got small. "No, now you listen to me. Don't you go pissing down my back and then tell me it's raining outside. You have to know *somethin'* about your husband, and if Yvie takes this to trial, and I hope to hell she will, you'll be called to testify, and it is your *duty*—"

"I don't know anything about my husband," Linda said coldly. Through her sunglasses she watched Karen-Lucie look out the window as though looking far into the distance; Linda saw the pretty eyes redden.

Karen-Lucie nodded slowly. Quietly she said, "Oh, child, of course. I am so sorry." She turned her gaze toward Linda, though her focus still seemed far away. "I am in no position to tell anyone how they ought to be cognizant and aware of what their husband is up to. I have thrown stones in a glass house, and I am sorry."

Almost always it's a surprise, the passing of permission to enter a place once seen as eternally closed. And this is how it was for a stunned Linda, who stood that day in that convenience store with the sun falling over packages of corn chips and heard those words of compassion—undeserved, for if Karen-Lucie had not known her husband's state of mind, Linda knew her own husband's state of mind too well—and sensed in them what would turn out to be true: that Yvonne Tuttle and Karen-Lucie would never return to town, there would be no trial, no mention of cameras, and Linda would live with her husband in a state of freedom, because he would always know, as they watched the news at night, took walks through the countryside, or sat in a restaurant and chatted, that his exemption from trouble was possibly or partly the result of his wife's discretion, and there would be no more women after that, the guestroom perhaps a sunny study neither would enter, a photograph of Karen-Lucie's cracked plates on the wall.

The essence of this Linda felt that day. She removed her

sunglasses to stare into the eyes of this woman; she wanted to reach for her hand. She even wanted—with a sudden surprising urgency—to caress her cheek, as though Karen-Lucie were the Pretty Nicely Girl who had suffered the blow from behind, who had come home from school and found her mother gone, thinking she had been important, loved all along.

The Hit-Thumb Theory

Waiting for her to arrive, Charlie Macauley watched from the window as twilight began to gather. Along the top of the soot-darkened wall of the parking area, barbed wire lay coiled, as though even the littered and unlovely motel lot posed such threat—or value—that it was immediately at war with the rest of the world. For Charlie, this seemed to prove the futility of the dreams presented in the department store windows he had walked by earlier, in this town they had found together, half an hour outside of Peoria: You could buy a snow blower or a nice wool dress for your wife, but beneath it all people were rats scurrying off to find garbage to eat, another rat to hump, making a nest in broken bricks, and soiling it so sourly that one's contribution to the world was only more excrement.

But there to the left was the top of a maple tree, the branches holding forth two pinkly yellow leaves with apologetic gentleness, and how had they held on until November? Right behind it was the last of the day's full light; generously, the colors from the setting sun sprayed upward over the open sky. Charlie put his large hand to the side of his face, remembering—why should this come to him now?—crouching on a small hillside, planting crocus bulbs with Marilyn in the same kind of autumn light. It had been their freshman year at the university. He remembered her eagerness: her eyes large with intent. He had known nothing about planting crocus bulbs, and these, she told him, short-breathed with excitement, would be her first. They had bought a trowel in town that afternoon, and walked up the small hill behind her dormitory to a patch of autumn grass next to the college woods. "Okay, here," she said, really anxious. He had seen how serious this was for her, planting her first flowers at the age of eighteen, with him, her first love— He had been moved by her eagerness, bundled up as she was in her long woolen coat; they dug the holes, put the bulbs in. "Bye, bye, good luck," she had said to one bulb. The very stuff that would make him roll his eyes now—her utter foolishness, the useless, nauseating *softness* that lay at the center of her—had thrilled him quietly that day with a rush of love and protectiveness as the autumn smell of earth filled him, kneeling there with the trowel. Dear, befuddled Marilyn, her face flushed with the excitement of the job done. "Do you think they'll come up?" she had asked worriedly. The poor thing, always worried. He said they would. And they did. A few did. But he could not remember that part as well. He could only really remember what he had long forgotten until right now: a day of innocence in autumn when they were just kids.

Charlie closed the window blinds. The blinds were plastic slats, dirty with age, and they clicked into place unevenly as he tugged on the cord.

Panic, like a large minnow darting upstream, moved back and forth inside him. He was suddenly as homesick as a child sent to stay with relatives: when the furniture seemed large and dark and strange, and the smell peculiar, each detail assaultive with a *differentness* that was almost unbearable. I want to go home, he thought. And the desire seemed to squeeze the breath from him, because it was not his home in Carlisle, Illinois, where he lived with Marilyn that he wanted to go home to, his grandchildren right down the street. And it was not his childhood home either, which was in Carlisle as well. Nor was it their first home as newlyweds outside of Madison. He did not know what home it was he longed for, but it seemed to him as he aged that his homesickness would increase, and because he could not tolerate the Marilyn he now lived with—a woman who nevertheless filled his estranged, expatriated heart with pity—he did not know what he would do, and the minnow darting through the stream of his anxiety landed briefly on his current Carlisle home with his grandchildren down the street, swam to the golf course where he did still sometimes enjoy the expanse of green before him, swam to the woman who might or might not show up here with her head of dark, glossy hair—and not one place seemed stable.

A soft knock came on his motel door.

"Hello, Charlie." She smiled, her eyes warm, as she walked past him into the room.

He knew instantly. His instincts had been honed in youth and this ability had never left him, the one to detect disaster.

Still, a man needed his dignity. So he nodded, and said, "Tracy."

She walked farther into the room, and when he saw that she had brought her overnight bag—and why would she not have, really?—he was pathetically and fleetingly gladdened, but then she sat on the bed and smiled at him again and he knew again.

"Take your coat?" he asked.

She shrugged her way out of it.

"Charlie," she said.

He watched himself. A little bit, it was fascinating. He was an organism about to be dealt a blow, and he used his natural powers to defend himself. This meant that he observed carefully the pitted parts of her upper cheeks, the pores that were jagged shapes indicating an adolescence he already knew had been hard. He noted the scent on the coat that he held, how even in its faintness it was cloying and unsubtle, and he hung the piece of clothing on the back of the desk chair rather than in the closet next to his own.

He observed the way her eyes would not look at him directly, and he thought that he hated dishonesty—or lack of courage—more than anything.

He moved as far away from her as the small room would allow, so that he stood leaning against the wall opposite.

Now she looked at him—with a sardonic, apologetic expression. "I need money," she said. And she sighed deeply, putting her hand on the bedspread. The fingers each had a ring, including her thumb, and it was still surprising to him how his mind was trying to remind him—Charlie, for God's sake, take note!—how repulsive so many parts of her *should be* to him and yet were not. The crap of class superiority would protect no man for long. Many lived whole lives and never knew this; Charlie did.

"Just tell me," he said.

"Ten."

He stayed exactly where he was. On the small table next to the bed his cellphone suddenly vibrated. Tracy leaned to look. "Your wife," she said, just reporting. Indifferent.

Charlie walked to the phone and slipped it into his pocket, where it shuddered in his palm a few moments before stopping. He said to Tracy, who remained sitting on the bed, "I can't, sweetheart."

"But you can." Clearly she had not expected this, and that was a surprise to him.

"No. I can't."

"You have plenty of money, Charlie."

"I have a wife and children and grandchildren, is what I have."

He had bought champagne because she liked it, and he watched as she noticed it now on the bureau top in the plastic motel bucket he'd filled with ice. She looked back at him ruefully. "You break my heart," she said. "Of all—"

He laughed, a bark of a sound. "Of all your johns I break your heart the most."

"But it's *true*." She stood and walked to the champagne. "And don't be crass, Charlie. I have clients, and you're not one of them."

"I know you have clients," he said.

"'Johns' is so . . . yesterday, for Christ's sake, Charlie."

"Forget it."

"No, I'm not forgetting it."

"Tracy, stop. You and I—right now—are about to act out one of the oldest stories in the book. And I don't care to. I know all the lines, I know all the background music. I don't want"—he opened his palm—"to do it, that's all. And I won't."

The pain that moved briefly across her face gratified him; he had always felt she loved him, as he did her. But there was suddenly a refreshing simplicity that seemed to move into the room, an unexpected and huge relief, a straightening out of—*things*. Go home and get your things in order, a doctor would say. No. *Affairs*. Go home and get your affairs in order. That clarification—he couldn't help it—struck Charlie as funny. He was, in the tiniest way, delighted, as though all those people whose lives had occurred long before he'd been born had known these things, phrases used for years: Go home and get your affairs in order.

Inside his pocket his phone vibrated again, and he brought it out to see. **Marilyn** was printed in blue across the screen.

"Want me to step out?" The question was intimate because it had been asked so many times in the past. The tone was conversational, familiar.

He nodded.

She slipped her coat back on, and he gave her a room key.

He said, "They have that tiny lobby—" But she said her car was fine, she'd listen to the radio, really, it was no problem. She had always been pretty wonderful that way. It was her job to be wonderful that way. But even after the day she'd told him her real name—sitting fully dressed in the chair by the desk, "I want to tell you my real name"—and brought out her driver's license to prove it, she was still wonderful that way. After the day she showed him her license, she'd insisted that he not offer her money again. Perhaps she'd been mulling this over, and now figured she was owed. Perhaps she was. The door closed quietly behind her. He resisted the urge to look through the blind slats and watch her get into her car.

The peculiar hopefulness had not left him, the pleasing understanding that the situation would be over soon, was—

essentially—over already. And it felt quite survivable, which he had somehow not known.

His wife was crying on the phone. "Charlie? Oh, I'm sorry to bother you, really I *am*. You're supposed to be having fun—well, I know it's not *fun,* but I mean I know it's your time, and—"

"What's happened?" He felt no alarm.

"Oh, Charlie, she was mean to me again. I called, you know, to see if the girls were all set with their Thanksgiving dresses, and Janet said to me, she said, 'Marilyn, I'm asking you, no, I'm telling you, I'm just going to come right out and tell you, Marilyn, that you call here too much. This is my house and Stevie is my husband, and we need some space.' That's what she said, Charlie. And Stevie, who even knows if he was home, does he have *any* spine, our son—"

Charlie stopped listening. He was absolutely and silently on the side of his children, and on the side of his son's wife. He sat down on the bed.

"Charlie?" she said.

"I'm here." Inadvertently he glanced at himself in the mirror. He had long ago stopped looking like anyone familiar.

In a few minutes he had calmed his wife enough to hang up. She'd apologized once more for disturbing him, and said he had made her feel better. He'd answered, "Okay then, Marilyn."

Alone in the room with silence he understood the previous hiatus, which had now returned to him, that spaciousness of calm: Long ago he'd assigned a private name to it. *The hit-thumb theory.* On his grandfather's roof as a child one summer, hammering tiles down hard, he'd discovered that if you hammered your thumb by mistake, there was a split second when you thought: Hey, this isn't so bad, considering how hard I was hit. . . . And *then*—after that moment of false, bewildered, and grateful relief—came the crash and crush of real pain. In the war this had happened so often, in so many forms, he'd sometimes thought he was brilliant—the analogy was that apt. In the war he had learned many things, and not one of them had he heard any psychologist mention during any of the meetings that Marilyn now thought he was attending.

✳

Charlie stood up. He felt the itch of desire that was carnal, corporeal; it included much and was not a stranger to him. Arms crossed, he walked back and forth in front of the queen-size bed with its spread that was made of fibers—he knew from having felt it many times—meant to endure all things. Back and forth he walked, back and forth. He had sometimes walked back and forth for hours. A warmth of emotion came to him.

He had not, at the time of its construction, been interested in the Memorial. No, Charlie Macauley had not been interested a bit. And yet one day—after many nights of being bombarded repeatedly with the memories of Khe

Sanh—he took a bus by himself all the way to Washington, and what a thing he found there. He had wept without sound or self-consciousness, walking along the dark granite wall, seeing names he recalled, touching them with his coarsened fingertips. And people nearby—he could sense them, tourists most likely—left him alone with respect; this he could feel, that they were *respecting* him as he wept! He had never thought such a thing possible.

Back in Carlisle he told Marilyn, "It was good I went." She surprised him by saying only "I'm glad, Charlie." And then later that night she said, "Listen. You go back whenever you need to, I mean it. We have enough money for you to make that trip any time you need it." People could surprise you. Not just their kindness, but also their sudden ability to express things the right way.

He felt he never expressed anything the right way.

Once he had been in a department store with his son and daughter-in-law; Janet had needed a sweatshirt. Charlie had just been following along, not interested one way or another. But his son was interested, and when Charlie glanced over, suddenly paying attention, he saw his son talking thoughtfully and earnestly to his wife—Janet was a plain and pleasant woman—and it was the glimpse of this, the engagement of his son in this small domestic exchange, that almost brought Charlie to his knees. What a son! What a man he was, this grown boy, who would stand so decently and discuss with his wife exactly what sweatshirt she desired in a store that smelled like a circus tent of cheap candy and peanuts and who knows what. His son caught his eye, his face opened. "Hey, Dad, how you doing there? Ready to go?"

The word arrived: Clean. His son was clean.

"I'm good," Charlie said, raising a hand slightly. "Take your time."

And because he was Charlie, who years ago had fouled himself profoundly, because he was Charlie and not someone else, he could not say to his son: You are decent and strong, and none of this has anything to do with me; but you came through it, that childhood that wasn't all roses, and I'm proud of you, I'm amazed by you. Charlie could not even say a watered-down version of whatever that feeling would be. He could not even clap his son on the shoulder in greeting, or when saying goodbye.

※

At the open door of the motel room, he stood gazing at the parking lot so she would know to return, and as she walked from the car toward him he was aware that she was aware of being watched—except he wasn't really watching her, because the smell of autumn had accosted him, the sudden chill, and that earthy, loamy fragrance came over him with something akin to excitement. Careful, he thought. Careful. He stepped back to let her enter.

Tracy did not remove her coat this time, and she sat in the chair by the desk instead of on the bed. He saw in her face that she had been preparing. "Please, Charlie. Now please just trust me. I *need* the money."

"I know you need it."

"Then please."

Perhaps perversely he was waiting to see if she would say he owed it to her, and then for the first time since he'd known her he saw her eyes fill with water. "Ah, Tracy. Tell me. Come on, babe, what is it?"

"My son."

Both very slowly, and immediately—this is how Charlie experienced it—he understood. Her son was in trouble with drugs. Owed a man ten thousand dollars. This knowledge entered the room like a large dark bird, its wingspan wide and frightening. He asked her directly.

She nodded, the tears coming down her cheeks then, coming, coming. He was oddly fascinated, having never seen her weep before, by the large tracks of mascara dripping onto her clothes, onto the turquoise-colored nylon blouse, the skirt of black, even her boots. His wife had never worn any makeup at all.

"Ah, Tracy. Kid, hey, sweetheart." He opened one arm to her, and believed he saw her desire to move to him, and maybe she would have, but he said, "Tracy, you're in danger yourself if you do this."

Something about that seemed to offend her deeply, and she shook her head and made fists with her many-ringed hands. "What the *fuck* do you know? You think you know shit—well, excuse-fucking-me, you don't know shit."

In this way she helped him. "I can't do it," he said, easily. "I can't withdraw ten thousand dollars from a bank account just like that—and not have Marilyn know. And I'm not going to, anyway."

Then her green eyes became like dark nostrils that flared, that is the image that came to him as he watched her: her eyes moving like the nostrils of a horse, pulled up, pulled back. "My son's going to be *dead* if I can't come up with this money." No tears now. Her breath came in little bursts.

Very slowly Charlie seated himself on the edge of the bed, facing her. Finally, quietly, he said, "You understand I had no idea you had a son."

"Well, of *course* I didn't tell you."

"But why not?" His question was genuine, puzzled.

"Let's see." She put a ringed finger to her chin in an exaggerated form of contemplation. "Because maybe if I explained the situation you'd think *less* of me?"

"Tracy, lots of people have kids in trouble." Her sarcasm bothered him. It seemed a knife abrading his arm. "I'd think *less* of you?" he echoed.

"Hah! That's right, how could you possibly think less of—"

"Stop it. *Goddamn* it. Stop it now. Stop it." He stood up.

She said quietly, "And you stop with the liberal white pity."

Just in time—but in time, always Charlie was just in time—he prevented himself from the slap across her face he could practically feel tingling throughout his hand. She turned from him with disdain, and so he did not apologize. Disdain did not become her; there was an element of theatricality to it, he felt.

There had been a chaplain. God, what a nice guy he was, simple. "God weeps with us," he had said, and you couldn't get mad at him for that. After the night at Khe Sanh they'd brought in another chaplain, a phony. Theatrical. "Jesus is your friend," the new chaplain would say, with silly pontification, as though he were dispensing Jesus Pills that only he was in charge of.

✳

Once he had gone to the hospital, and they had asked him to come back to attend a group. It was helpful, they suggested, to hear what others had to say. But it had included—oh, it made Charlie's head heavy to picture it—the circle of folding chairs, the younger ones in their fatigues, and it was mostly the younger ones who were there; they told of going into Iraqi towns, they told of not sleeping, they told of drinking too much, and Charlie could not stand them. Some were still young enough to have pimples. He had given *orders* to kids this young, and they made him sick to see. That horrified him: that he loathed these people. Being there with them exacerbated the very thing he thought he might die from, because he could tell—and he had feared this—that the fellow running the group did not *really* know what to do. Because there was nothing to do.

Talk about it. Sure thing. Take a cigarette break, talk about it more. At the third meeting he left when they broke for cigarettes, and then he was truly frightened.

Robin he met through her ad on the Internet. He drove the two hours from Carlisle to Peoria, and first greeted her in the lobby of the town's oldest hotel. The hotel had recently been refurbished, and the lobby sparkled with glass and waterfalls, the elevators pinged politely off to the right as he and Robin sat in the downstairs bar. They talked quietly, and he was, oh God almighty, he was the closest thing to happy he had been for years. A light-skinned black woman with green eyes, she gave off a sense of quiet self-assuredness; the lambency of this lightly worn authority made him right away love the space between her two front teeth, the kohl pencil line above her eyelashes, how she'd listen and nod and say, "That's right." She was forty years old, and she had two daughters who stayed with their grandmother when Robin could not be with them. He had taken a room on the top floor with a view of the river, and he noticed she discreetly kept an eye on her time, told him when he had gone over, added an hour, but she was smooth and calm and polite, and this quality remained even beneath the sweet outbursts of her sexuality, which, from the start, he had never felt to be faked, and so he was always able to feel okay. It was something.

"Why are you doing this?" he asked. "They must all wonder," he added.

"Some do, most don't. For money," she said, sitting up,

shrugging slightly. "That simple." The bumps of her spine lined up perfectly beneath her skin, and took his breath away.

It was her suggestion a few months later that they meet at the motel, a half hour from Peoria, that the money saved from not being in the fancy hotel could be used for them to see each other more. Only he couldn't see her more than he already was, he couldn't get away, so they had continued at the motel and he gave her the extra money, and then they fell in love—he had loved her, really, from the start, and she said she had fallen in love with him too, and told him her name was Tracy, while she sat fully clothed, right in that chair. And that was how it had been for seven months now: desperately in love. Charlie did not like desperate.

✳

Tracy was standing in the bathroom snapping tissues from the slit in the wall; from where Charlie sat on the bed he could see her yanking the stiff little skirts of white; the motel made sure you could not steal a box of them. She wiped her face, then washed it with a facecloth, reapplied lipstick, and returned to the room. His relief returned as well; it had never gone far. This was going to be over and that was all that mattered. And then Tracy—boy, how people could surprise you—said something insanely funny. She said, "I thought you had the character to help me out."

He asked her to repeat it, and she did, looking slightly

wary. He sat down on the bed and laughed and laughed. It was not a pleasant sound, and soon he was able to stop. "I miss it," he said, finally, wiping his sleeve across his face. She looked at him now with a faint sense of irritation. "Character," he added. "I miss it."

Those days seemed like ancient times, back when character was thought to mean everything, as though character were the altar before which all decency bowed. That science now showed genetics to be determinative just threw all that character stuff right over the waterfall. That anxiety was wired, or became wired after events of trauma, that one was not strong or weak, only made a certain way— Yes, he missed character! The nobility of it. Why, it was like being forced to give up religion once you'd been confronted with its base and primitive aspects, like having to view the Catholic Church with its nest of pedophilia and endless cover-ups and popes that worked with Hitler or Mussolini— Charlie was not Catholic, and the few Catholics he knew did continue to go to mass, but he could not see how, faced as they were with the chipping away of the brilliant façade; of course the Church was failing. But so was the Protestant concept of hard work and decency and character. Character! Who ever used that word anymore?

Tracy did. Tracy used that word. He looked over at her, the eyes still smudged black with that mascara. "Hey, kid," he said. "Hey, Tracy," and opened his arms to her.

Quietly she said, "My name isn't Tracy." After a moment she added, "And that license is fake. Just so you know.

The whole thing is fake." She leaned forward and whispered, "Fake."

A sound came from him. It was not unusual; he often made sounds without planning to. It happened sometimes in public, and it scared people. In a library once, a young person had looked at him, and Charlie understood that he had made a noise, a growl. Marilyn, idiot woman, whispered to the boy, "He was in the war."

And the kid didn't know what Marilyn meant.

Many young people did not know the name of the war he had served in. Was it because it was a conflict instead of a war? Was it because the country in its shame had pushed this war behind it like a child who in public was still being obstreperous, embarrassing? Or was it just the way that history went? He did not know. But when he heard a young person with those perfect teeth they all had now say, "Wait, what was that? I'm sorry—," followed by the self-deprecating grimace that was utterly false in its apology, trying to gauge how old Charlie was: "Sorry, uhm, was that in the first Iraq?" Then Charlie wanted to cry, he wanted to bawl, he wanted to bellow: "We did *that* and for what, for what, for what?"

He had never rid himself of an abiding dislike for all Asians.

And women who looked at him with fear.

"Here's an idea." Charlie stood up. "Let's go."

She hoisted her bag over her shoulder and waited. She did not look at him with fear. She did not look at him at all.

The hangers in the closet twanged against one another as he got his coat, metal hangers whose tops wrapped completely around the pole so they could not be stolen. "All set?" he asked in a cheerful voice, slipping on his coat, and he stood back to let her go through the door before him. There was the same familiar oddness of watching himself. The bewilderment of how much he loved her—yet that was more knowledge now than feeling—when not on any conceivable level did it make sense, except for the only one that mattered: She had saved him, given him the space within which he could breathe. Or he had, through her, given this to himself, because watching her he saw nothing—not one thing—that could have caused him to feel as he did; still desiring her, he found the sight of her puzzling. But it was over, praise God; there was still that open space of relief.

"Follow me in your car," he said.

He headed back toward the center of this town about which he knew almost nothing except for his forays to this motel. He knew the department store on Main Street and the Victorian-looking bed-and-breakfast that always had a VACANCY sign out front, yet always looked welcoming wearing its fresh color of pale blue like a shy child who had kindness within. He did not know where a branch of his bank might be, but he drove as though it would appear, only glancing once in the rearview mirror to see her following him; she was biting on her lip, a gesture so familiar to him he knew not to look in the mirror again. He drove with the fully set sun off to his right, and he noted once more that he felt okay. Passing an old church he thought that if she had not been following, he might have pulled over just to look at it from the road.

He had sometimes felt a need to pray. This need was as abhorrent to him as was the sight of his wife. He had been brought up in a Methodist church that had done nothing for him at all, except that he associated the experience with carsickness. He had attended some services at the Congregational church with Marilyn because she wanted to, but that experience of duty had attenuated as soon as the children reached early adolescence; he could not stand it, he told her, and she did not argue with him, they simply stopped going. And no one in the church pursued them. Except for the baptism of his grandchildren, and the funeral of Patty Nicely's husband, Charlie had not been in a church for years.

But these days, sometimes, he just wanted to go into a church and pray. He wanted to *fall on his knees,* and what would he pray for? Forgiveness. There was nothing else to pray for, not if you were Charlie Macauley. Charles Macauley did not have the luxury, the foolery, to pray for health for his children or the ability to better love his wife—no no no no no—Charlie Macauley could only pray, *beg on his knees,* Dear God, forgive me if you can stand to.

But how sickening. It made him sick.

Off to the right, past one more traffic light, he saw the sign for a branch of his bank. Pulling in to the parking lot he saw that the bank was still open and experienced a sense of strange accomplishment. He watched as she pulled in behind him; he signaled with one hand that she should stay where she was, and she nodded once. In about ten minutes he carried out two envelopes of cash—they had the bulky softness of flesh—and handed them to her through her partly open driver's side window. She opened the window more, as though she were about to thank him, but he shook his head to stop her. "If I hear from you again, I'll track you down and kill you myself," he said calmly. "Whether your name is Tracy or Lacy or Shitty or Pretty. Get it? Because you will need more."

She started her car and drove away.

Now the shaking began, first his hands, then his arms, and then his thighs. He had stolen from Marilyn, and wasn't that different? It seemed to him that that was different from anything else he had done. He was no longer earning money, nor was she. It really shook him up—he had stolen money from his wife. He sat in his car until he felt he could drive.

Only the faintest afterglow was in the sky now; it was a dangerous time, because it was essentially dark, not even dusk anymore; quickly, quietly, night had descended. And yet it was not nighttime. There were hours before one could sleep; his pills at best gave him five hours of sleep.

———

The bed-and-breakfast was a larger house than it appeared to be from the street. He parked in the lot behind it and walked back around—the air was crisp against his face like the witch hazel aftershave he'd used many years ago—and he went up the front steps, which slightly creaked, and that sound slightly pleased him. His instinct told him that this was a good place to be when the real blow arrived; he could be safe here, it could allow a man like him. In fact, the woman who answered the door was as old as he was, perhaps older, a tiny prim woman with good skin. Immediately he thought: She'll be afraid of me. But she did not seem to be. She looked him in the eye, asked if a room without a television would be all right. If he wanted to watch television, he could watch it here in the living room, the other guests seemed to have already turned in.

At first he told her no, he did not need a television, but when he saw his room, he understood that he could not sit in there and wait, and so he came back into the hall and she said, "Of course," and gave him the remote, and said, "Do you mind if I join you once I'm done in the kitchen?" He said he wouldn't mind. "I don't care what we watch," she added. In a distant way he understood that she had her own echoes of pain—at their age, he supposed, who did not? Then he supposed that many did not. It occurred to him often that many did not have echoes of pain from the silent noises he carried in his head.

He sat on the couch and heard her in the kitchen. He crossed his arms, and watched a British comedy because

British comedies were ridiculous, so removed from any-thing real—safe, those British comedies: the accents, the clackety teacups. And so he waited. It would come: the wave upon wave of raw pain after a blow like this, oh yes, it would come.

Quietly, the proprietress slipped into the room. From the edge of his eye he saw that she took the big chair in the corner. "Oh, perfect," she murmured, he assumed meaning the choice of show.

He wanted to ask her: If you made your name up and chose it to be Tracy, what do you think your real name would be?

And so it was coming closer, yes siree bob. He knew what it was, he had been there before, and then it would be over. And yet: It was taking longer than he thought it would.

You never get used to pain, no matter what anyone says about it. But now, for the first time, it occurred to him—could it really be the first time this had occurred to him?—that there was something far more frightening: people who no longer felt pain at all. He had seen it in other men—the blankness behind the eyes, the *lack* that then defined them.

So Charlie, a tiny bit, sat up straighter, and he stared pretty hard at that television set. He waited, hope like a crocus bulb inside him now. He waited and he hoped, he practically prayed. O sweet Jesus, let it come. Dear God, please, could you? Could you please let it come?

Mississippi Mary

"Tell your father I miss him," Mary said, dabbing at her eyes with the tissue her daughter handed her. "Can you tell him that, please? Tell him I'm sorry."

Her daughter looked up at the ceiling—such high ceilings in these Italian apartments—and turned to look briefly toward the window through which the ocean could be seen, then looked back at her mother. Angelina could not stop thinking how old her mother seemed, and small. And weirdly brown. She said, "Mom. *Please* stop this. Please stop it, Mom. It took my whole year's savings to fly over here, and I find you in this awful—I'm sorry, but it is—this squalid two-room flat with this guy, your husband, oh God. And he's almost *my* age, and we've just ignored that fact, what else could we do but ignore that fact? And now you're eighty years old, Mom."

"Seventy-eight." Mary had stopped weeping. "And he's not your age at all. He's sixty-two. Come on, honey."

Angelina said, "Okay, so you're seventy-eight. But you've had a stroke and a heart attack."

"Oh now please. That was years ago."

"And now you're telling me to tell Dad you miss him."

"I do miss him, honey. I imagine there must be days he misses me too." Mary's elbow rested on the arm of the chair; her hand waved the tissue listlessly.

"Mom. You don't get it, do you? Oh my God, you just don't get it." Angelina sat back on the sofa, brought both hands to her head, and pulled her fingers through her hair.

"Please don't yell, honey. Were you brought up to yell at people?" Her mother tucked the tissue into her large yellow leather pocketbook. "I never felt like I did get anything. No, there were lots of things I didn't get, I'll agree with you on that. Please don't yell at me though, Angelina. Did I just say that?" Mary's daughter, the youngest of five girls and Mary's (secret) favorite, was named Angelina because Mary knew during her pregnancy that she was carrying a little angel. Mary sat up straight and looked at the girl, who had been a middle-aged woman for years. Angelina did not look back. From where she sat in the corner chair, Mary could see the sun hitting the steeple of the church, and she let her eyes rest on that.

"Daddy yelled all the time," Angelina said, looking down at the upholstery of the couch. "You can't yell at me for yelling, and say I wasn't brought up that way, when I was—I was brought up with quite a yeller. Daddy was a yeller."

"Old yeller." Mary put a hand to her chest. "Honestly, what a sad movie that was. Why, we took you kids to see it, and I think Tammy didn't sleep for a month. Do you remember they took that poor dog out to the pasture and killed him?"

"They had to, Mom. He was rabid."

"A rabbit?"

"Rabid. Oh, Mommy, I don't want you to be making me sad like this." Angelina closed her eyes briefly, bouncing her hand gently on the couch.

"Of course you don't," her mother agreed. "Did you really spend all your savings to get here? Didn't your father help you at all? Honey, I wasn't yelling at you for yelling. Let's go do something fun."

Angelina said, "Everything in a foreign country seems so hard. And the Italians seem proud of not speaking English. Did you think that when you first came here? That everything seemed so hard?"

Mary nodded. "I did. But a person gets used to things. You know, for weeks if Paolo wasn't with me I didn't even try and get my coffee at that place on the corner. They thought I was his mother at first. And then they found out I was his wife and I think they were sort of laughing at us. But Paolo taught me how to pay with my coins on the plate."

"Mom."

"What, honey?"

"Oh, Mommy, it makes me sad. That's all."

"Not knowing how to put the right coins on a plate?"

"No, Mom. Thinking you were his *mother*."

Mary considered this. "Except why would they think I was his mother? I'm American, he's Italian. They probably didn't think that."

"You're *my* mother!" Angelina burst out, and this caused Mary to almost weep again, because she had a searing glimpse then of all the damage she must have done, and she, Mary Mumford, had never in her life planned on doing, or wanted to do, any damage to anyone.

⁂

They sat by the window in the café past the church; the café was built on rocks that looked out over the water. The late August sun sparkled crazily on everything. In four years, Mary had never stopped being banged on the head with the beauty of this village. But Mary was very anxious; her eldest daughter, Tammy, had emailed her that Angelina was having trouble in her marriage, and Mary had thought she would ask Angelina about this as soon as they were alone; yet she could not seem to do so. She would have to wait for Angelina to bring it up. Mary pointed to a large cruise ship on its way to Genoa, and Angelina nodded. The window they sat by was open, and the door was open. Mary ate her apricot cornetto, then put her hand on Angelina's arm; she started singing quietly "You Were Always on My Mind," but Angelina frowned and said, "Are you still wacky about Elvis?"

"I am." Mary sat up straight, putting her hands in her lap. "Paolo downloaded all his songs for me onto my phone."

Angelina opened her mouth, then closed it.

From the corner of her eye, Mary noticed once again that age had touched her baby; Angelina's face had creases by her mouth and by her eyes that Mary had not remembered. Her hair, still pale brown, and still worn below her shoulders, was thinner than Mary had thought it was. And the jeans she wore were so tight! Mary had noticed this right away. "Look, honey," Mary said, waving a hand toward the sea, "I just love how things are lived outside more in Italy. This open door, the open window."

Angelina said, "I'm cold."

"Take this." Mary handed her the scarf she always wore. "Unfold it," she directed, "and it will open enough to wrap right around your skinny little shoulder bones."

Her youngest child did this.

"Tell me about your life," Mary said. "The tiniest stuff, if you want."

Angelina rummaged through her blue straw handbag and brought out her phone, which she placed on the table between them. "Well, the twins and I went to a crafts fair, and you wouldn't believe what we got. Wait, I think I have a picture on my phone." Mary pulled her chair closer and peered at the phone, and she was able to see the pretty pink sweater that one of the twins had bought for Tammy's birthday.

"Tell me more," Mary said. Her desire seemed suddenly as large as the heavens. Show me, show me, cried her heart. "Show me *all* the pictures," she said.

"I have six hundred and thirty-two pics," Angelina reported, after squinting at her phone.

"Show me each one." Mary beamed at her sweet youngest girl.

"No crying," Angelina warned.

"Not a drop."

"One drop and we stop."

"My goodness," Mary said, thinking: Who was it that raised this girl?

✳

The sun went behind a cloud as they walked back to the caseggiato, and this changed the light dramatically. The day seemed suddenly autumnal, yet the palm trees and brightly painted buildings were at odds with this, even for Mary, who—presumably—should have been used to it. But Mary felt bewildered at all she had seen on her daughter's phone, all the life that was going on in Illinois without her. She said, "I was thinking of the Pretty Nicely Girls the other day. The Club, I guess I was remembering The Club and the dances there."

"The Pretty Nicely Girls were sluts." Angelina said this over her shoulder.

"No they were not. Angelina. Don't be silly."

"Mom." Angelina stopped walking and turned to her mother. "They were sluts. At least the oldest two were. They totally slept with everyone."

Mary stopped walking as well. She took her sunglasses off and looked at her daughter. "Are you serious?"

"Mom, I thought you knew that."

"How in the world would I know that?"

"Mom, *everyone* knew it. And I told you at the time. My God." Angelina added after a moment, "Patty wasn't, though. I think she wasn't."

"Patty?"

"The youngest Nicely girl. She and I are friends now." Angelina pushed her sunglasses up on her nose.

"Well, that's nice," Mary said. "That's *nicely*. How long have you been friends?"

"Four years. She works with me."

Four years, thought Mary. Four years, I have not seen my dearest little angel. Glancing at her daughter, Mary thought again that the girl's jeans were too tight across her little bottom. She was a middle-aged woman, Angelina. Was Angelina having an *affair*? Mary shook her head slowly. "Well, I was thinking of them when they were little girls, the Pretty Nicely Girls. Your father and I went to the wedding of one of them. They had the reception at The Club."

Angelina had started walking again. "Do you ever miss it?" She asked this over her shoulder. "The Club?"

"Oh, honey." Mary felt winded. "No, I can't say I miss The Club. It was never my thing, you know."

"But you guys went there a lot." A small gust of wind raised Angelina's hair so that the ends rose above her shoulder, straight up.

"We did." Mary followed her daughter up the street, and after a moment Angelina turned to wait for her. "That one wall they had, filled with Indian arrowheads under glass, I don't know," Mary said.

"I didn't know you didn't like it," her daughter said. "Mom, *my* wedding reception was held there."

"Honey, I said it wasn't my thing, and it wasn't. I wasn't raised that way and I never got used to it, all the showing off of new dresses and the women so silly." Oh dear, Mary thought. Uh-oh.

"Mom, don't you remember Mrs. Nicely? You know, what happened to her?" Angelina, her eyes blocked by her sunglasses, looked at her mother.

"No. What happened to her?" Mary asked; trepidation came and nestled on her chest.

"Nothing. Come on, let's go."

"Hold on a minute," Mary said. She stepped into a tiny shop and Angelina squeezed in behind her. The man behind the counter said, "Ah, buongiorno, buongiorno." Mary answered in Italian, pointing to Angelina. The man placed a pack of cigarettes onto the tiny counter before him. Mary said, "Si, grazie," and then something more that Angelina did not understand, and the man opened his mouth in a huge smile, showing teeth that were stained, some missing. He answered her mother quickly. Her mother turned, her huge yellow leather pocketbook bumping into Angelina. "Honey, he says you're beautiful. Bellissima!" Her mother spoke to the man again, and they went back onto the street. "He says you look like me. Oh, I haven't heard that in ages. People always used to say, She looks like her mother."

"Mom, you're still smoking?"

"My one cigarette a day, yes."

"I used to love it when people said I looked like you," Angelina said. "Are you sure the one cigarette a day is okay?"

"I'm not dead yet." Mary was about to say: I'm very surprised I'm not dead yet. But she had warned herself not to speak of her death to Angelina.

Angelina tucked her arm into her mother's and her mother pulled her out of the way of a woman on a bicycle. "Mom," Angelina said, turning to look, "that woman is *your* age, and she's smoking, and she has her pearls tossed over her neck, and she's wearing high heels, and she's pedaling her bike with a basket of stuff in the back."

"Oh, I know, honey. It just amazed me when I came here. Then I figured it out—the women are just versions of people pulling up to Walmart in their cars. Only they're on a bike."

Angelina yawned hugely. Finally she said, "Everything's always amazed you, Mom."

✳

Inside the apartment, Mary lay down on her bed, this was her afternoon rest, and Angelina said she'd email her kids. Through the window Mary could see the sea. "Bring your computer in here," she called to her daughter, but Angelina called back, "You rest, Mom, I'm okay. We'll skype with them later."

Please, Mary thought. Please come in here and be with me. Because the fact that her youngest daughter—her *favorite,* the only one of her children who had not seen her for four years, who had refused to see her!, although the girl had said she would come a year ago—the fact that this girl (woman) was now in the next room of the apartment gave a feel of naturalness to Mary's life, and yet it was not natural to have this child here, at all. Please, Mary thought. But she was tired, and the Please could also be for Paolo to have a good time with his kids, whom he was visiting right now in Genoa, or a Please that her other girls would stay healthy, oh there were many things Mary could say Please for—

Kathie Nicely.

Mary edged up onto an elbow. The woman who had walked out on her family. A flash of heat shot through Mary, even as she remembered the woman: petite, pleasing-looking. "Huh," Mary said quietly, and lay back down.

Kathie Nicely, behind her smile, had not cared for Mary, and only now did Mary understand that it was because Mary had come from such humble beginnings. "Humble beginnings" is what Mary's mother-in-law had said of Mary's background. It was true. They didn't have two nickels to rub together. But Mary had been a cute little thing, a cheerleader, when she caught the eye of the Mumford boy, whose father had that huge business in farm machinery. What had she known? Lying on her bed, Mary shook her head. Less than nothing she had known.

Well, she thought, turning on her side, she knew some things now: the fact that Kathie Nicely had never really acknowledged her. Mary waved a hand dismissively. But they had gone to one of the girls' weddings. The oldest girl? It must have been. Years ago.

Wait. Wait. Wait.

It came to Mary now. Kathie Nicely had already moved out, and people at the wedding were whispering that she'd had an affair. And somehow—why would this be the case?—it was this, the whisperings, that had caused Mary to understand that her own husband had been having an affair—with that dreadful fat Aileen, his secretary. It had taken a few days to get the confession from him, then Mary had her heart attack— Well, of course she hadn't remembered Kathie Nicely when her own world had tumbled down around her so.

———

She reached across the bed and tugged her yellow leather pocketbook toward her, found her phone, and put her earbuds in; Elvis sang "I've Lost You." Two years older than Mary, and from the same little town in Mississippi that Mary had been born in, Elvis Presley had always been her secret friend, though she had never once seen him, whisked off as she was to the farmlands of Illinois when she was just a baby so that her father could take a job in a filling station owned by his cousin in a town called Carlisle. One time, Elvis performed two hours from where she lived, but with the children so little she could not go to see him. Oh, Mary had spent more time thinking about Elvis than anyone could have imagined, and in this way the pleasure of her mind—because it was her mind and could not be known by others—had developed early in her marriage. In her mind, she had been backstage with Elvis; she had looked into his lonely eyes and let him see that she understood him. In her mind, she had consoled him about the "fat and forty" remark that the stupid comedian had made on national television; in her mind, they had spent time alone while he talked to her of his hometown and his mama. When he died, she wept quietly for days.

But Paolo—she had told Paolo of her fantastical life with Elvis, and Paolo had watched her, one eye partially closed, then he opened his arms and hugged her. The freedom. Oh God, the freedom of being loved—!

She woke to see her daughter in the doorway. Mary patted the bed beside her. "Come, honey. That's not his side, I'm on his side."

Angelina placed her shiny little computer on the dresser top and went and lay down beside her mother. Mary said, "Look at that ocean. It goes all the way to Spain." Angelina closed her eyes. Mary sat up a bit. "Say, how's your father's brain?" She belched softly, the apricot filling of her earlier cornetto returning on her.

"He's not demented," Angelina said, "though I watch out for it."

"Good," Mary answered. She found a tissue in her large yellow pocketbook and touched it to her lips. "I meant his cancer, though."

Angelina opened her eyes and sat up herself now. "There's no recurrence of the cancer. Don't you think we'd have told you?"

"I don't know," Mary answered truthfully.

"We're not *mean,* Mom. We'd tell you if Dad got sick again. Come on, Mom."

"Angel, of course you're not mean. No one said you were mean. I was just asking." Mary thought: I am a fool. This clarity of belief made her feel sorry for her daughter and weepy again. She sat up farther. "Come on, let's not think about it." From her yellow leather pocketbook she pulled out a plastic bag of used tissues and dropped them into a wastebasket beneath the table by her bed.

Angelina laughed. "You're so funny. Your constant collection of used tissues."

And this made Mary laugh—to hear her sweet child laughing. "I've told you, when you have five girls and they're all home sick with colds, you have to just keep walking around picking up tissues—"

"I know, Mom. I *know*." Angelina put her head on her mother's arm, and her mother, with her other hand, briefly touched her daughter's face.

※

Who leaves a marriage after fifty-one years? Not Mary Mumford, that's for sure. She shook her head. Angelina asked, "What, Mom?" Mary shook her head again. They were still lying on the bed. Who leaves a marriage after fifty-one years?

Well—Mary did. She waited until all five girls were grown, she waited until she recovered from the heart attack she'd had when she found out about the secretary her husband had been having an affair with for thirteen years— thirteen years with that woman who was *so fat*—then she waited while she recovered from the stroke she had after her husband found the letters from Paolo—almost ten years ago now—oh, he had yelled, red in his face, that awful vein on the side of his head just about to burst, but it burst in *her* instead, she supposed that was part of the marriage, she took on his bursting veins, and then she waited until he did not die of the brain cancer he seemed to get right after she told him she was leaving him; so she waited and waited and dear Paolo waited as well—and so—here she was.

How did you ever know? You never knew anything, and anyone who thought they knew anything—well, they were in for a great big surprise.

"You were so good to me." Angelina slipped off her flat black shoes while still lying down; they fell to the floor with soft sounds.

"What do you mean, honey?"

"You were so good to me, Mom. You put me to bed until I was *eighteen*."

"I loved you," Mary said. "I still love you."

"This *is* your side of the bed, right?" Angelina sat up.

"Yes, honey, I promise."

Angelina sighed and lay down next to her mother again. "I'm sorry. I'll be nice to him when he's back tomorrow. I know he's nice, Mom. I'm being a baby."

Mary said, "I'd feel the same way if I were you," but she thought this was not true. She glanced at the clock and said, "Come on. It's time for my swim."

Angelina got off the bed, smoothed her hair over one shoulder. "You're so brown," she said to her mother. "It's funny to see you so brown."

"Well, it's the seaside." Mary went into the bathroom and put her bathing suit on, and put a dress on over it. "Let's go. Now, you don't have to do anything in the water but sit. It just holds you up, I swear."

At four o'clock the sun was vastly bright and the houses built up high on the hills were lit by it, the pale colors, the bright yellow flowers, the palm trees. Mary walked in her plastic shoes across the rocks and down to the beach. She pulled her dress off, put it on her towel, found her goggles.

"Mom, you're wearing a *bikini*."

"A two-piece, honey. Look around. Do you see one person wearing a one-piece? Except for you?" Mary put her goggles on and walked into the water, in just a moment she pushed off and paddled along, seeing the small fish below her. Every day when she swam, that was her favorite part of the day, and it was now, even with her daughter here to visit. Splashing made her stop. Angelina was there, her hair wet. "Mom, you're so funny. In your yellow bikini. And your goggles. Oh my God, Mom!" So they swam and laughed and the sun sliced down on them.

Sitting on a sun-warmed rock, Angelina said, "Do you have friends?"

"I do." Mary nodded. "Valeria is my main friend. Didn't I write to you about her? Oh, I love her. I met her in the square. I'd seen her sitting by an old lady—why, she, Valeria, has the sweetest face, Angelina, the sweetest face I've ever seen. Other than your own. She was sitting by the sea with an old woman who had legs that were dark with about one hundred years of sun. I just stared at that woman's legs, the veins were purple inside these dark, *dark* encasings, like sausages, really, and I thought: What a miracle life is! These old legs still pumping up blood. I was thinking this, and then I glanced at the woman who was talking to her. Tiny little thing, Valeria is, almost sitting on her lap, and the sweetness of her face— Why—" Mary shook her head. "And then by the church two days later, this tiny lady walked right up to me. She knows some English, I know a little Italian. Yes, I have a friend. You can meet her; she'd love to meet you."

"Okay," said Angelina. "Maybe in a few days. I don't know."

"Whenever you want."

Four ships were in front of them, one a cruise ship headed toward Genoa, the others tankers.

"Is he nice to you, Mom?"

Mary said, "He's very good to me."

"Okay, then. All right." In a moment Angelina added, "And his sons? And their wives? Are they nice to you too?"

"Perfectly fine." Mary waved a hand dismissively. "Look what Paolo's done for me, honey. He downloaded all of Elvis's songs onto my phone." Mary reached for her phone, looked at it, then put it back into her big yellow pocketbook.

"You told me," Angelina said. And then, in a nicer tone, Angelina added, "You've always liked yellow." She touched her mother's pocketbook. "And this is *yellow*."

"I have always loved yellow."

"And your yellow bikini. You crack me up, Mom."

Another ship, far out on the horizon, appeared. Mary pointed to it, and Angelina nodded slowly.

✳

She ran a bath for Angelina, like she had done for years, and she almost wondered if the girl would let her stay and talk, as she often did when she was little. But Angelina said, "Okay, Mom. I'll be out soon."

Lying on her bed—where she spent much of her days— Mary looked at the high ceiling and thought that what her daughter could not understand was what it had been like to be so famished. Almost fifty years of being *parched*. At her husband's forty-first birthday surprise party—and Mary had been so proud to make it for his forty-first so he'd be really surprised, and boy he *was* really surprised—she had noticed how he did not dance with her, not once. Later she realized he was just not in love with her. And at the fiftieth wedding anniversary party the girls threw them, he did not ask her to dance either.

Later that year her girls had given her the birthday gift, she was sixty-nine, of going to Italy with a group. And when the group went to the little village of Bogliasco she became lost in the rain, and Paolo found her, and he spoke English, and she did not really think too much about his age. She fell in love. She did. He'd been married for twenty years, it had seemed like fifty to him, and now he was alone—they were both *parched*.

But she thought of her husband, her ex-husband, more often these days. She worried about him. You could not live with someone for fifty years and not worry about him. And miss him. At times she felt gutted with her missing of him. Angelina had not yet mentioned her own marriage, and

Mary was waiting with real apprehension for her to do so. Angelina's husband was a good man; who knew? Who knew.

✳

In the bathtub, Angelina put her head back and smeared her hair with shampoo. She had been happy, swimming with her mother. But now, sitting in this horrible old tub on its clawed feet, trying to hold the odd little shower hose so water didn't get everywhere, now Angelina felt the worst feeling of all, that of not being able to believe things. She could not believe that her mother looked so different. She could not believe that her mother no longer lived ten miles from her, from her grandchildren. She could not believe that her mother was married to a boring Italian man as young as Tammy. No, she wanted to cry, soaping her hair, No no no! *Oh,* she had missed her mother terribly. Day after day, week after week, she had talked of her mother incessantly, and Jack had listened, but then Jack had finally and suddenly left, saying, You're in love with your mother, Angie, you're not in love with me. And so she had come here to see her mother now, to tell her about her marriage: this woman—her mother—that she was in love with.

To have the pleasant-faced Paolo pick her up at the airport, standing next to this small, old, brown woman, her mother (!), driving them here along these crazy roads, so *what* if he went to spend a few nights with his son in Genoa so Angelina could have time alone with her mother? Angelina hated everything about this place, the beauty of the dumb village, the high ceilings of this awful apartment, the arrogance of the Italians. In her mind now she pictured her youth, the long stretches of acres of corn beside their home in Illinois. Her father was a yeller, true. And he'd had that stupid relationship with that stupid fat woman for thirteen years, true too. But that was just pathetic, in Angelina's eyes—painful, of course, but pathetic. Why couldn't her mother see what she had done by leaving? Why couldn't she see it? There could be only one reason: that her mother was, behind her daffiness, a little bit dumb; she lacked imagination.

Boo-hoo. Boo-hoo. This is what her father used to say to any of them when he found them crying, putting his face right up to theirs. He really was a mean snake of a man (but he was her father, and she loved him), in favor of guns and shooting anyone who came into your house; he'd been raised that way, and had he had sons instead of daughters they might have been like that too. Angelina hoped he never got himself to Italy, to this awful little village, to find this nothing of a man Paolo who had taken her mother's affections away from them so very late in life. If her father was sick again, really and truly going to die this time, he'd somehow get himself to this village, find this nothing of a Paolo, and shoot him in public and then shoot himself.

It sounded almost Italian, the craziness of it.

"Why did you think Daddy would help me with the

money to get here?" She asked her mother this as she sat on the bed and toweled her hair dry.

"He's your father. I stand by what I said." Mary gave one nod.

"Why would he help me come see his ex-wife who left him in the middle of brain cancer?"

Inside her head, Mary felt the kind of electrical twang that meant she was suddenly very angry. She sat up straight, her back against the bed's headboard. "I did not leave him when he had his brain cancer. That was the whole point. Good God, did you kids not know that? I stayed and took care of him, and when he got better I went on with my life." She thought: I'm going to have another stroke, young lady, if you don't stop this nonsense. But Angelina was not a young lady, she had two children almost ready to leave home, and she'd be sensitive because of whatever was happening to her— But Mary was very angry. She had never liked being angry; she didn't know what to do with it. "What's the story with Jack?" she asked. "You haven't mentioned him once."

Angelina looked at the floor. After a moment she said, "We've had a hard time. We're working on things. We never learned how to fight." She glanced unpleasantly at her mother, then looked at the floor again. "You and Daddy never fought. Well, Daddy yelled and you let him. But I wouldn't call that constructive fighting."

Mary waited. Her anger did not leave her; it had sharpened her wits. She felt coherent, strong. "Constructive fighting," she said. "Your father and I did not fight constructively. I see, go on."

"I don't want to talk about it." Angelina was still looking at the floor, absolutely moping. The child could have been twelve years old, sulking, yet Angelina had never been a sulker.

"Angelina." Mary felt her voice shake with anger. "You listen to me. I have not seen you in four years. The other kids have all come to see me, and you have not. Tammy even came here twice. Now, I know you're angry with me. I don't blame you." Mary sat up so her feet were on the floor. "Wait. I do blame you."

With alarm, Angelina looked up at her mother.

"I blame you because you're an adult. I didn't leave you when you were a child. I did everything I could, and then— I fell in love. So go ahead and be angry, but I wish, I wish—" And then Mary's anger left her; she felt terrible. She felt absolutely awful at how Angelina looked. "Say something, honey," Mary said. "Say anything."

Angelina said nothing. It did not occur to Mary that her daughter did not know what to say. For many minutes they were silent, Angelina staring at the floor, Mary staring at her child. Finally Mary spoke. She said quietly, "Did I ever tell you that when the doctor handed you to me, I recognized you?"

Angelina looked at her then. She shook her head slightly.

"It didn't happen with the others. Oh, I loved them immediately, of course. But it was different with you. When the doctor said, 'Take your daughter, Mary,' I took you and I looked at you, and it was the strangest thing, Angelina, because I thought, Oh, it's *you*. It didn't even seem surprising. It felt like the most natural thing in the world, but I recognized you, honey. I don't understand why I recognized you, but I did."

Angelina walked to her mother's side of the bed and sat next to her. Angelina said, "Tell me what you mean."

"Well, I looked at you and I thought—this is exactly what I thought, honey—Oh, it's you, of course it's you. That's what I thought. I just knew you, but it was more that I *recognized* you." Mary touched her daughter's hair, still damp and smelling of shampoo. "And when I was carrying you, I knew I was carrying—"

"A little angel." Angelina spoke the words with her mother. They were quiet for a while, sitting on the edge of the bed, holding hands. Mary eventually said, "Do you remember how you loved those books about that girl on the prairie? And then we saw it on television too?"

"I remember." Angelina turned to her. "Mostly, though, I remember how you put me to bed. Every night. I couldn't bear you to leave. Every night I'd say, Not yet!"

Mary said, "Sometimes I'd be so tired I'd lie down right next to you, and if my head went below yours you couldn't stand it. Do you remember that?"

Angelina said, "It was like you became the child. I needed you to be the grown-up."

Mary said, "I understand." Again they were silent. Then

Mary said, holding her girl's wrist, "Don't tell your sisters how I recognized you when you were born, and how I didn't recognize them—I don't like secrets. But *you* should know."

Angelina said, sitting up straighter, "Then it must mean—"

"We don't know what it means," her mother said. "We don't know what anything means in this whole world. But I know what I knew when I saw you. And I know you have always made me so happy. I know you are my dearest little angel." (She did not say, and only fleetingly did she think: And you have always taken up so much space in my heart that it has sometimes felt to be a burden.)

❋

In the kitchen, while they found the pans and pots and boiled the water and heated the sauce, Mary was close to ecstatic. Happiness thrummed through her—she could eat it like bread! To be in the kitchen with her girl, to speak of ordinary things, the children, Angelina's job as a teacher—oh, it was wonderful. She turned the lamps on in the dining space and they ate the pasta and talked of Angelina's sisters. A glass of wine in her and Mary said, "My word, what you said about those Nicely girls. My goodness."

"Oh." Angelina wiped her mouth with her napkin. "Want to hear some gossip?"

"Oh *yes*," said Mary.

"Remember Charlie Macauley? Come on, you have to remember him."

"I do remember him. He was tall, a nice man. Then he went to Vietnam. Boy, that was so sad."

"Yes, that's him. Well, it turns out he'd been seeing a prostitute in Peoria, all the while telling his wife that he was going to a veterans' support group thing. Wait, wait— Well, apparently he gave this prostitute ten thousand dollars and his wife found out and she kicked him out."

"Angelina."

"She did. She kicked him out. And guess who he's with now? Come on, Mom, guess!"

"Angel, I can't."

"Patty Nicely!"

"No."

"Yes! Okay, Patty won't come *right* out and tell me, but she's lost weight, did I tell you she'd gained weight and the kids at school call her Fatty Patty? Well, she's certainly been *very* nice to Charlie, she looks wonderful, and they were friends anyway, kind of. So there you go." Angelina gave her mother a meaningful nod. "You never know."

"My goodness," Mary said. "Angel, that is *wonderful* gossip, my word. They call her Fatty Patty, the kids at school? To her face?"

"No. I don't think she even knows. Just once." Angelina sighed, pushing her plate back. "She's awfully nice."

———

When they finished eating, Mary went and sat on the sofa. She patted the place next to her and Angelina joined her, bringing her wineglass with her. "Listen to me," Mary said. "Listen to what I have to tell you."

Angelina sat up straight and looked at her mother's feet. She felt that only now did she see that her mother's ankles were no longer tiny, as they had always been.

"You were thirteen. I came to pick you up at the library. And I yelled at you—" Mary's voice suddenly quavered, and Angelina looked at her, saying, "Mommy—" But her mother shook her head and said, "No, honey, let me go on. I only want to say I yelled at you, I really *yelled* at you, I have no idea what about, but I yelled and you were frightened, and I was yelling because I had found out about your father and Aileen, but I never told you about that—until, well, you know, a million years later, but the point is, honey, I frightened you, I *yelled* at you, and you were frightened." Mary looked past Angelina toward the window, and her face moved. "And I am so, so sorry," she said.

After a moment, Angelina asked, "Is that it?"

Mary looked at her. "Well, yes, honey. I've felt terrible about it for years."

"I don't remember it. It doesn't matter." But Angelina thought she did remember, and inside her now she cried, Mom, he was a stupid pig, but so what, Mom, please, Mom—*Please don't leave, Mommy!* After many moments, Angelina said, "Mom, it was so long ago, that stuff with Aileen. Did you leave Daddy because of that? Because it sure took you long enough." She could hear the coldness of her tone. It was as if the wine had turned on her; she felt that cold toward her mother, suddenly.

Mary said thoughtfully, "I just don't know, honey, but I think I would not have left."

"We've never talked about it at all," Angelina said.

Her mother was silent, and when Angelina looked at her she was stabbed by the look of sadness on her mother's face. But her mother said, "Well, tell me, honey. Now that you're finally here. Tell me what it's like for you. I told you before, I fell in love with Paolo. Your father and I were not compatible in many ways, but, honey—I fell in love. So now you tell *me*."

Angelina said, "He's a bank teller, Mom. And this place is—" She looked around. She wanted to say "squalid" again, but it was not that. It just was not—it was not lovely—and it was a strange place with its high ceilings and chairs that were worn in their upholstery.

Her mother sat up very straight. "This place is beautiful," she said. "Why, we have the view of the water. We'd never have been able to afford it if Paolo's wife hadn't had money."

"She had money?"

"She *has* money, some. Yes. And he's like me, he didn't come from much."

Angelina said nothing.

Mary continued, "The point is this. I am comfortable with him. I am in love with him, and I am *comfortable* with him. Your father's family, as you very well know, had money, and your father has been very successful. Frankly, Angelina, I don't give a damn about money. I like not having it, in fact. Except that not having it keeps me from seeing you."

"You've returned to your roots." Angelina meant this sarcastically, but she thought it sounded silly.

"My father worked at a filling station. We had nothing. You know that. Paolo does not have money and he does not have huge ideas of how to make it. If that's what you mean by returning to my roots."

Angelina stared at her own feet stretched out in front of her; her ankles were thin. "Wait." She looked up at her mother. "So he lived here with his wife?"

"That's right. She met someone and took off, and she left him this place, and we're glad to have it."

"I don't understand anything," Angelina said finally.

"No. I don't either."

Mary reached for her daughter's hand. And yet to Mary came the sudden knowledge—how stupid she had been not to see this before—that her daughter would never forgive her for leaving her father. Not in Mary's lifetime. And Mary's lifetime was not very long anymore. But the knowledge was terrible—and yet in Mary's head was that twang again, she was angry—!

Please.

Angelina said, "Mom. I don't want you to die. That's the whole thing. You took from me the ability to care for you in your old age, and I wanted to be with you if you died, when you die. Mom. I wanted that."

Mary looked at her, this woman with the creases by her mouth.

"Mom, I'm trying to tell you—"

"I know what you're trying to tell me." And now Mary had to be careful. She had to be careful because this girl-woman was her daughter. She could not tell her—this child she loved as much as she had loved anything—that she did not dread her death, that she was almost ready for it, not really but getting there, and it was horrifying to realize that—that life had worn her out, worn her down, she was almost ready to die, and she would die, probably not too long from now. Always, there was that grasping for a few more years, Mary had seen this with many people, and she did not feel it—or she did, but she did not. No. She felt tired out, she felt *almost* ready, and she could not tell her child this. And she also felt terror at the thought. She pictured it—lying here in this very room while Paolo rushed about—and she was terrified, because she would not see her girls again, she would not see her husband again, and she meant their father, that husband, she would not see all of them again and it terrified her. And she could not tell her daughter that had she known what she was doing to her, to her dearest little Angel, she might not have done it.

But this was life! And it was messy! Angelina, my child, please—

"You didn't even take the money Dad owes you from the divorce—in the state of Illinois, you could have had some money."

Mary said, "But, honey." She paused, looking for the words. Finally she said, "When you fall in love you get into some"—Mary waved a hand upward—"bubble or something. You don't *think*. But why should I have his money? I never earned a penny of it."

Angelina thought, You're a dope, Mom.

Mary shook her head slowly and said, "I'm a dope."

Angelina said, "Well, if you had taken the money, I could visit you, that's one thing you could have done with it."

Mary said, "I understand that. Now."

"And why do you say you didn't earn it? You raised five girls, Mom."

Mary nodded. "I always felt that I was at the mercy of your father and his family. Like I was a kept woman. I should have had a job. But why would I have had a job? I don't know what you and Jack have done about finances, but I'll tell you, Angelina, it's a good thing you've always worked. It makes things a lot more fair between two people."

Angelina said, "Jack's going to come back."

"Jack *left*? I didn't know he'd left." Mary pulled back to look at her daughter.

Angelina said, "I don't want to talk about it, but things were my fault too. So he's coming back. When I get home."

"He *left*?"

"Yes. And I don't want to talk about it."

But Mary was really frightened now; her chatty little Angel, who used to tell her everything, all the nights putting her to bed, the baths drawn—whoosh, it was gone, gone! "Honey," she said after a moment, "it's none of my business, but was there another woman?"

Angelina looked at her mother with a sudden stoniness. "Yeah." And then in a moment she added, "You."

"What do you mean?" Mary said.

"I mean, the other woman was you, Mom. I couldn't get over your leaving. I couldn't stop talking about you. And Jack said I was in love with my mother."

"Oh, honey. Oh dear God," said Mary.

"He left over a year ago, and I was going to come see you last summer, but he kept saying he might come back, so I stayed home, but now he really *is* going to come back."

Angelina allowed her mother to take hold of her, and Angelina wept on her mother's chest. She wept for a long time. Every so often she made a sound of such terrible pain that Mary felt removed from it. Finally, Angelina lifted her head, wiped at her nose, and said, "I feel better now."

They sat together on the couch for many minutes, Mary's arm around her girl. Mary ran her other hand over Angelina's leg. Then Mary said, "You know, when I first saw you in these jeans I thought maybe you were having an affair."

Angelina sat up straight. "What?" she said.

"I didn't know it was with me."

"Mom, what are you talking about?"

Mary said, "Well, honey, these jeans are kind of tight for a woman your age, and I just thought—you know, maybe—"

Angelina began to laugh, though her face was still wet. "Mom, I bought these jeans special for this trip. I thought women in Italy wore— I thought they wore sexy things."

"Oh, the jeans are sexy," Mary said. She didn't think they were sexy at all.

"You don't like them?" Angelina looked ready to cry again.

"Honey, I *do*."

And then Angelina—oh, bless her soul—began to really laugh. "Well, *I* don't like them. I feel like a jerk in them. But I bought them special, so you'd think I was, you know, sophisticated or something." Angelina added, "In my *one-piece* bathing suit!" Both of them laughed until they had tears in their eyes, and even then they kept on laughing. But Mary thought: Not one thing lasts forever; still, may Angelina have this moment for the rest of her life.

✳

Mary said that she was going out to sit in the courtyard by the church and have her evening smoke. In fact, Mary had not had a cigarette since she'd moved here. She had told the man in the shop that the cigarettes were for her daughter.

"Okay, Mom," Angelina said, and her mother went and got her yellow leather pocketbook. In a few minutes, Angelina looked from the window and saw that her mother was sitting on a bench that overlooked the town, and also the sea. She sat beneath a streetlamp, and Angelina could just make out that her earbuds were in, her head moving slightly up and down, a cigarette held to her lips. Then Angelina saw a woman come up to her mother, and Angelina realized it must be Valeria; how happy her mother seemed to see her! Her mother stood, and she and this tiny woman kissed each other on one cheek and then the other, and Angelina watched her mother's hands gesticulating; at one point she held the cigarette toward her friend and they both laughed. Then the small woman reached up and they kissed on each cheek again, and the small woman went away and Angelina's mother sat down again. She sat there on the bench, took two more long puffs on her cigarette, then squished it against the ground, but she held the butt and carefully placed it in a small plastic bag she took from her large yellow pocketbook.

Angelina could not stop staring at her, her mother who sat very still, looking out at the water. And then Angelina saw her mother suddenly rise and walk into the street. An old man was crossing, he was weaving—not with drunkenness, it seemed, but with some malady of age. It was surprising to Angelina how quickly her mother moved to him; in the light from the streetlamp Angelina saw the old man's face, and it was not just the way he smiled up at her mother, it was the humanness of his expression, the warmth and depth of his appreciation, and as her mother helped him across the street, Angelina saw then her mother's face briefly in the light as well. Perhaps it was the angle of the light, but her mother's face had a momentary brilliance upon it—as Angelina saw her mother take the man's hand, saw her mother help this man across the street; and when they got to the other side they appeared to speak briefly to each other, and then her mother waved as the man went down the sidewalk. Angelina thought, Now she will come back upstairs.

But her mother sat down once again on the bench; she put her earbuds back in, and her head began moving up and down to whatever she was listening to on her phone, it would have to be an Elvis song. She was facing the sea, and seemed to be gazing out at the boats with their lights on.

Her mother had read to Angelina all the books about the little girl on the prairie, and when there was a television show about it she would watch the show with Angelina, the two of them curled up on the couch together. Her mother had told Angelina about how they killed the Indians, took their land. Her father had said they deserved it; her mother had told her they did not deserve it, but that is what happened. People always kept moving, her mother had said, it's the American way. Moving west, moving south, marrying up, marrying down, getting divorced—but moving.

Her mother had recognized her the moment she was born—

"Okay, Mommy," Angelina whispered. She stepped away from the window and went to the bedroom to get her computer, but she sat on the bed instead, looking around, this bed her mother shared with a man named Paolo.

For eighteen years her mother had put her to bed. Don't leave yet, Angelina would say, not yet! Her father, from the doorway, would say, 'Night, Lina, go to sleep. Now Angelina gazed through the window at the sea; it was dark, the ships had their lights on. She heard her mother coming up the stairs. And she knew, Angelina knew, that she had seen something important when her mother helped the man who was unsteady crossing the street. Briefly—it would be brief, Angelina knew this, she knew she would always be the child—but briefly a ceiling had been raised; she pictured her mother's quick and gracious loveliness to that man on the street: A street in a village on the coast of Italy, her mother, a pioneer.

Sister

Pete Barton knew that his sister Lucy was coming to Chicago for her paperback book tour; he followed her online. Only in the last few months had he had the house wired for Wi-Fi, and he had bought himself a small laptop computer, and what he most liked watching was what Lucy was up to. He felt a sense of awe that she was who she was: She had left this tiny house, this small town, the poverty they had endured—she'd left it all, and moved to New York City, and she was, in his eyes, famous. When he saw her on his computer, giving speeches to auditoriums that were packed with people, it gave him a quiet thrill. His *sister*—

Seventeen years it had been since he had seen her; she had not been back since their father died, although she had been to Chicago any number of times since then—she had told him this. But she called him most Sunday nights, and when they spoke he forgot about her being famous and just talked to her, and he listened as well; she'd had a new hus-band now for a number of years, and he heard about that, and she sometimes spoke of her daughters, but he didn't care about them so much—he did not know why. But she seemed to understand this, and just spoke of them briefly.

When his telephone rang on Sunday night—a few weeks after he'd learned about her Chicago tour—Lucy said to him, "Petie, I'm coming to Chicago, and then I'm going to rent a car on that Saturday and drive to Amgash to see you." He was astonished. "Great!" he said. And as soon as they hung up he felt fear.

He had two weeks.

During that time his fear increased, and when he spoke to her on the Sunday in between, and he said, "Really glad you're coming to see me," he thought she'd have an excuse and say it wouldn't work out. Instead she said, "Oh, me *too*."

So he set about cleaning the house. He bought some cleaning stuff and put it in a pail of hot water, watching the suds, then he got down on his hands and knees and scrubbed the floor; the grime there amazed him. He scrubbed the kitchen counters, and was amazed by their filth as well. He took down the curtains that hung in front of the blinds and washed them in the old washing machine. In his mind they were blue-gray curtains, but it turned out that they were off-white. He washed them a second time, and they were an even brighter off-white. He cleaned the windows, and no-ticed that their streaking was on the outside as well, so he went outside and cleaned the windows from there. In the late August sun they seemed to still have streaky swirls when he got done. He thought he might keep the blinds down, which is what he usually did anyway.

But when he stepped through the door—the only door to the house, which opened right into the small living room and the kitchen area to the right—he saw things the way she would see them, and he thought: She will die, this place will depress her so much. He really didn't know what to do. He drove to the Walmart outside of town and bought a rug, and that made a huge difference. Still, the couch was lumpy and its original yellow flowered upholstery was worn; at points it was threadbare. The kitchen table had a linoleum top, and it was impossible to make it look newer. There was no tablecloth in the house, and he had doubts about buying one. He gave up. But the day before she was to arrive he went into town and got a haircut; usually he cut his own hair. Only when he was driving home did he wonder: Was he supposed to have tipped the man who cut his hair?

That night he woke at three with nightmares he could not remember. He woke again at four, and could not get back to sleep. She had said she'd be there by two in the afternoon. At one o'clock he opened the blinds up, but even though the sky was cloudy the windows still looked streaky, and so he closed the blinds again. Then he sat on the couch and waited.

✳

At twenty minutes past two, Pete heard a car in the pebbly driveway. He peeked through the blind and saw a woman step from a white car. When he heard the knock on the door, he was so anxious he felt his eyesight had been affected. He had expected—he realized this later—that sunlight would flood the house, meaning that the presence of Lucy would shine and shine. But she was shorter than he remembered, and much thinner. And she wore a black jacket that seemed like something a man would wear, and black jeans, and black boots, and her face looked so tired. And old! But her eyes sparkled. "Petie," she said, and he said, "Lucy."

She held her arms out, and he gave her a tentative hug; they had never hugged in their family and the gesture was not easy for him. The top of her head reached his chin. He stepped back and said, "I got a haircut," moving his hand over his head.

"You look wonderful," Lucy said.

And then, almost, he wished she hadn't come; it would be too tiring.

"I couldn't find the road," Lucy said, and her face showed real surprise. "I mean, I must have driven by it five times, I kept thinking, Where *is* it? And then finally—God, I'm so stupid—finally I realized the sign's been taken down, you know, the sign that said 'Sewing and Alterations.'"

"Oh yeah. I took that sign down over a year ago." Pete added, "I figured it was time."

"Oh, of course it was, Petie. It's just my stupid old mind

kept waiting to see it—and I— Hello, Pete. Oh my God, hello." She looked straight into his eyes, and he saw that it was her; he saw his sister.

"I cleaned up for you," he said.

"Well, *thank* you."

Oh, he was nervous.

"Petie, listen to this." She moved to the couch and sat down with a familiarity that surprised him, as though she had been sitting on that couch for years. He sat slowly in the old armchair in the corner, and watched while she slipped off her black boots, which were more like shoes, he saw now. "Listen to this," Lucy said. "I saw Abel Blaine. He came to my reading."

"You saw Abel?" Abel Blaine was their second cousin on their mother's side; he had come to stay with them a few summers when they were children, along with his younger sister, Dottie. Abel and Dottie had been as poor as they were. "What was he like?" Pete had not thought of Abel for years. "Wow, Lucy, you saw *Abel*. Where does he live?"

"I'll tell you, hold on." Lucy scooted her feet up under her, leaning down to push aside her black shoe-boots. Pete had never seen anything like them. Little zippers went up their backs. "Okay." Lucy brushed at the front of her black jacket and said, "So, I'm sitting there signing books, and this man—this tall man with nice-looking gray hair—he was standing very patiently, I noticed that, all alone, and when he finally got to me he said, 'Hi, Lucy,' and his voice sounded familiar, can you believe that, Pete? After all these years, he *sounded* like Abel. And I said, 'Wait,' and he said, 'It's me, Abel,' and I just jumped up, Petie, and we hugged, oh God did we hug. Abel Blaine!"

Pete felt excited; her excitement made its way right to him.

Lucy said, "He lives right outside of Chicago, in kind of a ritzy neighborhood. He's been running an air-conditioning outfit for years. I said, 'Is your wife here?,' and he said, No, she was sorry she couldn't make it, but she had some auxiliary meeting or something."

"I bet she just didn't want to come," Pete said.

"Exactly." Lucy nodded vehemently. "You're so right, Petie, how did you know that? It was just sort of obvious to me, I mean, it *seemed* like he was lying, and I don't think Abel could ever really tell a lie."

"He married a snob." Pete sat back. "That's what Mommy said years ago."

"Mom told me that too, way back when I was in the hospital and she came to visit me." Lucy tugged her black jacket closed. "She said that Abel had married the boss's daughter, that she was a hoity-toity. He was dressed very well, you know, an expensive suit."

"How could you tell it was expensive?" Pete asked.

"Well, right." Lucy nodded meaningfully. "Petie, it has taken me years to figure out what clothes are expensive, but— Well, you can just tell after a while, I mean, the suit fit him perfectly and was made from nice cloth. But he was *so* glad to see me, Petie, oh, you would have died."

"How's Dottie?" Pete leaned his elbows onto his knees, and glancing around briefly he realized that there were no pictures on the walls. He seldom sat in the chair he was sitting in now, and so he must never have noticed. He always sat where Lucy was sitting, facing the door. The walls just hung there, plain and off-white.

"He says Dottie's good. She owns a bed-and-breakfast outside of Peoria, in Jennisberg. No kids. But Abel has three kids. And two little grandchildren. He seemed *very*"—Lucy slapped her knee lightly—"*very* happy about those grandchildren."

"Oh, Lucy. That's nice."

"It was nice. It was just wonderful." Lucy ran her fingers through her hair, which partly—toward the front—went to her chin and was a pale brown. "Oh, and guess who I saw in Houston? I was signing books, and this woman—I really wouldn't have recognized her—but it was Carol Darr."

"Oh, right." Pete sat back; the bare walls seemed to be darker in the corners. "Yeah, the Darr girl. She moved away. She lives in Houston?"

"Carol was in my class, Petie, and she was so mean, oh, that girl was so mean to me."

"Lucy, everyone was mean to us."

For some reason this made them look at each other, and they briefly—almost—laughed.

"Yeah," said Lucy. "Oh, well."

"Was she mean to you in Houston?"

"*No.* That's what I was going to tell you. She actually

seemed shy when she introduced herself. Shy! And so I said, Oh, Carol, how nice to see you. And she waited for me to sign her book—what could I sign for her? So I just wrote 'Best wishes,' and then I gave her the book, and she leaned down toward me and said quietly, 'I'm really proud of you, Lucy.' And I said, 'Oh, thank you, Carol.' I don't know, Petie, I think she's grown up and probably feels a little bad. I'm just saying that's the impression I got."

"Was she married?" Pete asked.

Lucy held up a finger. "I don't know," she said slowly. "No man was with her, but maybe she had one at home." Lucy looked over at her brother. "Don't know." She gave a little shrug. Then she patted the lumpy couch next to her and said, "Petie, tell me everything, please tell me how you are! Here I am, just two minutes inside the house, blab-blab-blabbing about myself."

"That's okay. I like hearing it." And he did. Oh, he was happy.

"Petie, why don't you get a dog? You always liked animals." Lucy looked around, as though really looking for the first time. "Have you ever had a dog?"

"No. I've thought about it, but when I go to work it would be alone all day and that makes me too sad."

"Get two dogs," Lucy said. "Get three." Then Lucy said, "Pete, tell me more what you mentioned on the phone. You work at a soup kitchen? Tell me more about that."

"Yeah, okay," Pete said. "You remember Tommy Guptill?"

Lucy sat up straight, putting her feet on the floor; her socks were two different colors, Pete noticed, one brown and one blue. She said, "The janitor at school. What a nice man he was."

Pete nodded. "Well, we're kind of friends now, and I go with him and his wife once a week and work at the soup kitchen in Carlisle."

Lucy shook her head appreciatively. "That's a wonderful thing for you to do. Petie, that just makes me really proud of you."

"Why?" He really couldn't think why.

"Because not everyone can work in a soup kitchen, and it just makes me proud that you do. How long has there been a soup kitchen in Carlisle?" Lucy plucked something from the leg of her jeans and flicked it into the air.

"A few years now. I don't know. But I've been going for a couple months," Pete said.

"Is Tommy well? He must be old." Lucy looked over at Pete.

"He's old," Pete said. "But he's still going strong, and his wife is too. They ask about you sometimes, Lucy. I bet they'd love to see you." He was surprised by the change of her face; it closed down.

"No," she said, "but you tell them I said hi." Then Lucy said, "Look, just so you know, I called Vicky and said I would be here, and she said she was busy today. It's okay. I get it."

Pete said, "She told me that too, and I'm kind of mad at

her for it, Lucy. I mean, she's your sister." Without meaning to, Pete wiped a finger on the wall near him, and dust came off, a dark streak of it.

"Oh, Petie," said Lucy. "Look at it from her point of view. I leave, I *never* come back, plus she asks me for money—did you know that? Well, she does, and I always give it to her, she can't make much working in that nursing home, and you know, her husband was laid off, and she must feel, you know, however she feels. Do you see her? Is she happy? Well, I know she's not *happy*, but I mean—is she okay?"

"She's okay." Pete wiped the dust streak onto his jeans.

"Okay." And then Lucy looked straight ahead, as though she was thinking about something hard. After a moment she just shook her head, and looked at Pete again. "Awfully nice to see you," she said.

"Lucy, I need to ask you something."

"What?"

He thought he saw alarm cross her face. He said, "Was I supposed to tip the guy who cut my hair? I always cut it myself. But I went in Carlisle to that barbershop, and the guy cut my hair, and whisked that little apron thing off me, and I paid him, and I've been worried since. Was I supposed to tip him?"

"Does he own the shop?" Lucy tucked her feet up beneath her again.

"I don't know."

"Because if the guy *owns* the place, you don't have to tip

him, but if he doesn't own it, you should." Lucy waved a
hand dismissively. "Don't worry about it. If you go back,
tip him a few dollars, but don't worry about it."

He loved her for this, for her knowledge of the world
and her knowledge of him. She didn't seem embarrassed
that he had asked such a question. Oh, he really was happy!
Maybe that was why he didn't hear the car in the driveway.
He heard only the loud knock on the door, and he and Lucy
both jumped. He saw her fear; she sat up straight and her
face became stern; he felt the fear himself. He put his finger
to his lips and leaned over to—very, very carefully—pull
back the tiniest part of the blind. "Oh," he said. "Oh, it's
Vicky."

✳

The clouds had moved away and the sun was shining down
now; the cornfields were spread out beyond. As Pete stood
at the open door, he suddenly realized that Vicky was fat.
He had known this without knowing it, but now that he
saw her standing at the door, he saw that she was really
pretty fat. It had to do with how tiny Lucy was, that he saw
this now. Vicky wore a flowered shirt and navy blue pants—
they must have had an elastic waistband around her big
stomach—and she held a red pocketbook; her glasses had
slipped partway down her nose. They nodded in greeting,
and she stepped past him. Pete stood for another moment
gazing out at the cornfields; in the afterimage in his mind,

something had looked different about Vicky's face. When he turned to go back inside, Lucy was standing, but she sat down again, and Pete figured that she had tried to give Vicky a hug and that Vicky would have none of it; this is what he saw in Vicky's expression.

"What is that?" Vicky said, pointing at the rug.

"Oh, it's a rug," Pete said. "I bought it the other day."

"Doesn't it look nice?" Lucy asked.

Vicky stepped around it and stood in front of Lucy. "Well, here you are," she said. "So why don't you tell me— what in this great wide world has brought you back to Amgash?"

Lucy nodded, as though she understood the question. "We're old," Lucy said, looking up at her sister. "And we're getting older."

Vicky dropped her pocketbook onto the floor and then sat down on the couch as far away from Lucy as she could. But Vicky was big and she couldn't get that far away, the couch was not very large. Vicky sat, her almost-all-white hair cut short, with a fringe around it, as though it had been cut with a bowl on her head; she tried to hoist a knee up over the other, but she was too big, and so she sat on the end of the couch, and to Pete she looked like someone in a wheelchair he had seen in Carlisle when he went to get his hair cut, an older woman, huge, who was sitting in a motorized wheelchair that she drove around.

But then he saw: Vicky had on lipstick.

Across her mouth, curving on her upper lip and across

her plump bottom lip, was an orangey-red coating of lipstick. Pete could not remember seeing Vicky wear any lipstick before. When Pete looked at Lucy, he saw that she had no lipstick on, and he felt a tiny shudder go through him, as though his soul had a toothache.

"So, like, we're going to die soon and you thought you should come say goodbye?" Vicky asked this, looking directly at her sister. "You look dressed for a funeral, by the way."

Lucy crossed her legs and put her hands, splayed together, over her knee. "I wouldn't put it that way. That we're going to die soon, I mean."

"How would you put it?" asked Vicky.

Lucy's face seemed to grow pink. She said, "I would put it the way I just put it. That we're old. And we're getting older." She gave a tiny nod. "And I wanted to see you guys."

"Are you in trouble?" Vicky asked.

"No," said Lucy.

"Are you sick?"

"No." Lucy added, "Not that I know of."

And then there was a silence that went on for a long time. In Pete's mind the silence became very long. He was used to silence, but this was not a good silence. He moved back to the armchair in the corner and sat down slowly, carefully.

"How are you, Vicky?" Lucy asked this, looking over at her sister.

"I'm fine. How are you?"

"Oh God," Lucy said, and she put her elbows on her knees, covering her face for a moment with her hands. "Vicky, please—"

Vicky said, " 'Vicky, please'? '*Vicky,* please'? Lucy, you left here and you have never once come back since Daddy died. And you say to me, 'Vicky, please'—as though I'm the one who's done something wrong."

Pete wiped his finger across the wall again, and again his finger became streaked with dust. He did it twice more before he spread his hands over his knees.

Lucy said, looking upward, "I've been very busy."

"Busy? Who isn't busy?" Vicky pushed her glasses up her nose. In a moment she added, "Hey, Lucy, is that what's called a truthful sentence? Didn't I just see you on the computer giving a talk about truthful sentences? 'A writer should write only what is true.' Some crap like that you were saying. And you sit there and say to me, 'I've been very busy.' Well. I don't believe you. You didn't come here because you didn't want to."

Pete was surprised to see Lucy's face relax. She nodded at her sister. "You're right," she said.

But Vicky wasn't done. She leaned forward and said, "You know why *I* came over here today? To tell you—and I know you give me money, and you never have to give me another cent, I wouldn't take another cent, but I came over here to see you today to tell you: You make me sick." She sat back and wagged a finger toward her sister; on her wrist was a watch whose small leather band seemed squished into her flesh. "You do, Lucy. Every time I see you online, every time I see you, you are acting so nice, and it makes me sick."

Pete looked at the rug. The rug seemed to holler at him, *You are such a dope for buying me.*

After a long time, Lucy said quietly, "Well, it makes me sick too. What I'd really like to say on whatever you're watching—and why are you watching me?—what I'd really like to say, sometimes, is just: Fuck you."

Pete looked up. He said, "Wow. Who do you want to say that to?"

"Oh," Lucy said, running a hand through her hair, "usually it's some woman who doesn't like my work and stands up and says so. Or some reporter who wants to know about my personal life."

Pete asked, "A person really stands up and says they don't like your work?"

"Sometimes."

Pete moved his chair slightly forward. "Then why don't they just stay home?"

"Well, that's my point." Lucy opened her hand, waved it in a small gesture. "Fuck them."

"Poor Lucy," said Vicky, and her voice was sarcastic.

"Yeah, poor me," Lucy said, and sat back.

"Mommy's favorite," Vicky said, and Lucy said, "What?"

"I said you were her favorite kid, and boy did that pay off, for *you.*"

Lucy looked at Pete and then she said, "I was her favor-

ite?" Her surprise surprised Pete. "I was?" she asked, and
he shrugged. Lucy said, "I didn't know she *had* a favorite."

"That's because you didn't know anything that went on
in this house, Lucy. You stayed after school every day, and
she let you." Vicky was looking at her sister; her chin was
quivering.

"I knew plenty of what went on in this house." Lucy's
voice had hardened. "And she didn't let me, I just did it."

"She let you, Lucy. Because she thought you were smart.
And she thought *she* was smart." Vicky tugged hard on the
bottom of her blouse; Pete could see a strip of her flesh
exposed above her pants, almost bluish.

Pete said, "Hey, Vicky. Lucy saw Abel. Lucy, tell Vicky
about seeing Abel."

But when Lucy said, "I saw Abel," Vicky only shrugged
and said, "I couldn't stand his sister, Dottie. Mom always
made her a new dress."

"Well, Dottie was poor," Lucy said.

"Lucy, *we* were poor." Vicky leaned forward, as though
trying to put her face in front of Lucy's face.

"I know that," Lucy said. She suddenly stood and walked
to the front window. She gave the blind cord a little tug, and
it opened up. Sunlight spilled into the room. She walked to
the other window and opened that blind as well. Then Pete
saw that the dirt from the floor had been scrubbed into the
corners, it was right there to see in this sunlight.

"Do you ever eat?" Vicky asked this to Lucy, and Lucy
shook her head before she sat back down on the couch.

"Not much," Lucy said. "Appetite I do not have."

"Me either," Pete said. "I just know when I have to eat because I start to feel funny in the head." The sudden sunlight—golden in its early autumnness—was too much for Pete, he really wanted to close the blinds. It was like an itch, and he had to work hard not to do it.

"It's strange," said Vicky, and her voice was no longer belligerent. "It's odd, isn't it? That you two would be so skinny and I'd be the one who eats all the time. I don't remember you guys having to eat out of the toilet, but maybe you did. Who knows." Vicky took a deep breath that caused her cheeks to pop out, and then she sighed hugely.

Pete thought to himself: Don't do it. And what he meant was, Don't get up and close the blinds.

After a moment Lucy said, "What did you say?"

Vicky said, "Oh, one time when we had meat." Vicky scratched hard at her neck. "It was liver. God, did I hate the taste of that. Mommy thought we should be having— I don't know—red blood cells or something, and she'd gotten a slab of liver from someone, and it was so awful, I put the pieces in my mouth and went and spit in the toilet, and the stupid, *stupid* toilet didn't flush, and they found the pieces swimming in it and—"

"Stop," Lucy said, raising her hand, palm outward. "We get it."

Vicky seemed irritated by this. "Well, Lucy, you and Petie had to eat from the garbage whenever you threw food away, I can remember right there"—and she pointed with her fin-

ger, thrusting it twice, to the area where the kitchen was—
"you'd have to kneel, and pick out whatever food you'd
thrown away, and eat it right from the garbage, and you'd
be crying— Okay, okay. Look, I'm just saying I can understand why you guys wouldn't want to eat. I just don't understand why I *do*."

Lucy reached and rubbed her sister's knee. But to Pete
the gesture seemed obligatory, as though Vicky was a kid
and had said something embarrassing that the grown-up,
Lucy, was going to pretend didn't happen.

"How's your job?" Lucy asked Vicky.

"My job is a job. It stinks."

"Well, I'm sorry to hear that," Lucy said.

Pete glanced at the wall where the streaks of dust had
come off; it was a mess of smudges.

"Another true sentence, I'm sure." Vicky hoisted herself
up to more of a sitting position. "But you know, a funny
thing happened there just the other day. This old lady
named Anna-Marie, she's been in a wheelchair since I
started there years ago, and she has never said a word in all
those years, people say, Oh, Anna-Marie can't talk anymore, and she just wheels around in her chair banging into
people. And the other day I was standing at the nurses' station and all of a sudden I feel my hand being held. And I
look down and there's Anna-Marie in her wheelchair, and
she says to me with a big smile, 'Hi, Vicky.'"

Hearing this made Pete feel happy. He felt the happiness
move through him like a warm liquid.

Lucy said, "Vicky, that's a wonderful story."

"It was sweet," Vicky acknowledged. "And sweet things never happen there, I can tell you."

Pete suddenly remembered something. "Vicky," he said, "tell Lucy about Lila. How she's going to go to college."

"Oh." Vicky scratched at her neck again; a red streak appeared across it. Then she looked carefully at her fingers. "Yeah. My baby girl is probably going to college next year." She looked up at Lucy. "Her grades are good and her guidance counselor says she can get her into college with expenses paid. Just like you did, Lucy."

"Are you *serious*?" Lucy sat forward. "Vicky, that's so exciting."

"I guess so," Vicky said. She pushed on her bottom lip with her fingers, biting it.

"But it is," Lucy said.

Vicky took her hand away from her mouth, rubbed it on her pants. "Sure. And then she'll just go away like you did."

Pete saw Lucy's face change, as though she'd been slapped. Then Lucy said, "No, she won't."

"Why won't she?" Vicky tried to rearrange herself on the couch. When Lucy didn't answer, Vicky said, in a slightly mincing voice, "Because she has a different mother, Vicky. That's why she won't. Thank you, Lucy."

Lucy closed her eyes briefly.

"You know who her guidance counselor is?" Vicky looked back around at Pete. "Patty Nicely. She was the youngest of the Pretty Nicely Girls, remember them?"

Lucy said, "That's who's helping get her to college?"

"Yup. 'Fatty Patty,' the kids call her. Or they used to, she's lost some weight," Vicky said.

"They call Patty Nicely 'Fatty Patty'?" Lucy frowned at Vicky.

"Oh yeah, sure. You know, they're kids." Vicky waited and then she said, "They call me 'Icky Vicky' at work."

"No, they don't," Lucy said.

"Yes, they do."

Pete said, "You never told me that, Vicky. Well, they're old and they've gone dopey-dope in their heads."

"It's not the patients. It's the others who work there. I heard this woman say, two days ago she said this, Here comes Icky Vicky." And Vicky took her glasses off; tears began to roll down her face.

"Oh, honey," said Lucy. She moved closer to her sister, she rubbed her knee. "Oh, that's disgusting. You are *not* icky, Vicky, you're—"

"I am *so* icky, Lucy. Just look at me." Tears kept coming from Vicky's eyes. They rolled down over her mouth, with its lipstick.

"You know what?" Lucy said. She stopped rubbing Vicky's knee and started patting it instead. "Cry away. Honey, just cry your eyes out, it's okay. My God, do you remember how we were *never* supposed to cry?"

Pete leaned forward; he said, "Lucy's right. You just go ahead and cry. No one's going to cut your clothes up this time."

Vicky looked over at him. "What did you say?" She wiped at her nose with her bare hand. Lucy brought a tissue from her jacket pocket and handed it to Vicky.

Pete said, "I said, No one is going to cut your clothes up. Never again."

Vicky said, "What are you talking about?"

Pete said, "Don't you remember how one day you were here crying and Mommy came home and cut up your clothes?"

"She *did*?" Lucy said.

"She did?" Vicky was patting the tissue over her face; she patted it lightly on her mouth. "Oh, wait. Oh my God, she did. I'd forgotten about that." Vicky looked at Lucy, then at Pete; her face without its glasses seemed younger, and bloated. "Why would she do that?" Vicky asked this with wonder.

"Wait," Lucy said. "Mom cut up your *clothes*?"

"Yeah." Vicky nodded slowly. "I'd been crying, I can't remember why. It had to do with something that had happened at school, and I was just crying and crying—you're right, Lucy, they just hated for us to cry, but they weren't home, so I was sitting here crying, and, Pete, you were here—and I was crying so hard I didn't hear her come in. Oh, I do remember this now." Vicky waved the tissue in her hand; there were reddish spots on it from her lipstick. "And she came through that door and she said, 'Stop that noise right now, Vicky,' but you know, I couldn't—quite. And she said, 'I said stop that noise right now,' and then she went and got her shears from the sewing area and she went in our room—and I just remember hearing the hangers moving, and then it was you, Pete"—Vicky touched the tissue to her face again, turning slightly in Pete's direction—"who figured out what she was doing, and you went and stood by the door of the room, and then I got up and stood behind you and I screamed, Mommy, don't, oh, don't, Mommy! And she just kept cutting up my clothes and tossing the pieces on the floor and on the bed. Then she walked out and went upstairs." Vicky just sat now, staring at the floor. "Oh my God," Vicky said. "She hated me—so—much."

"But she *sewed*," Lucy said. "Why in the world would she cut up your clothes?"

"Oh, she sewed them back together the next day. On her machine." Vicky lifted a hand listlessly. "She just stuck the pieces together and sewed them, so I looked like, I don't know, I looked like even more of a moron." Vicky said this, gazing in front of her.

After a long moment, Pete said, still leaning forward in his chair, "Look, you guys, I've been thinking about her a lot recently, and here's what I think: I think she just wasn't made right."

His siblings said nothing for a long while. Then Lucy said, "Well, maybe. And then she had Daddy to contend with." Lucy added, "She was gritty, though."

"What do you mean?" asked Vicky.

"She had grit. She hung in there."

"What was she supposed to do? She didn't have anywhere to go." Vicky looked at the bottom of her blouse, and tried to tug it down again.

"She could have left us. She'd have made money with her sewing. Just for herself. But she didn't." Lucy said this, then pressed her lips together.

"You know what I hated the most?" Vicky glanced at Lucy and Pete, and said almost serenely, "The sex sounds. When Daddy wasn't walking around twanging his wang, they'd be doing it right up there—" She pointed to the ceiling. "And it made me sick to hear it, the bed shaking, and the *sounds* he made. I never heard any man make the sounds he made during sex." She blew her nose. "Boy, try having a normal sex life after all that crap for years."

Pete said, "I never did. Try, I mean." His face became hot quickly; oh, he was embarrassed. But Vicky smiled back at him, and he added, "I know what you mean, though. My bedroom was right next to theirs, and jeepers—" He shook his head quickly, more like a shiver. "It was like I was in there with them."

Vicky said, "Wait. You know what? *He* made all the sounds; there was never a sound from her."

Pete had never thought about this before. "Hey, you're right," he said. "You're right. She never did make any sounds."

"Oh God," Vicky said, and she sighed. "Oh, the poor—"

"Stop," Lucy said. "Let's just stop this. It doesn't do any good."

"But it's true," said Vicky. "It's all true, who else are we supposed to talk to about this? Lucy, why don't you write a story about a mother who cuts up her daughter's clothes? You want truthful sentences? I mean it. Write about that."

Lucy was putting her shoes back on. "I don't want to write that story." Her voice sounded angry.

Pete said, "And who'd want to read it?"

"I would," Vicky said.

"I still like to read about the family on the prairie," Pete said. "Remember that series of books? I have them upstairs."

"I can't," Lucy said. "I can't."

"So don't write it," Vicky said, with a shrug, "I was just saying— Oh my God, I remember now—"

Lucy stood up. "Stop it," she said. Her face had two red splotches high on her cheeks. "Stop it," she repeated. "Just stop it." She looked at Vicky, then she looked at Pete. She said—and her voice was loud and wobbly—"It was *not* that bad." Her voice rose. "No, I mean it."

Silence hung in the room.

In a few moments, Vicky said calmly, "It was exactly that bad, Lucy."

Lucy looked at the ceiling, then she began to shake her hands as if she had just washed them and there was no towel. "I can't stand it," she said. "Oh God help me. I can't stand it, I can't stand it, I can't—"

And then Pete understood that she could not stand the

house, or being in Amgash, that she had become frightened, the way he had been frightened to get his hair cut, only Lucy was so much more frightened than that.

"Okay, Lucy," he said. He stood up and went to her. "Just relax now."

"Yes," Lucy said. "Yes. No. I don't know what to do. I don't know—" It seemed she was panting. "You guys," she said, looking from one to the other, and her eyes were blinking hard. "I don't know what to *do*. Help me, oh God—" She kept shaking her hands, harder and harder.

"Lucy," said Vicky. She hoisted herself up from the couch and walked over to her sister. "Now you just get hold of yourself—"

"I can't," Lucy said. "I can't. I just can't— Oh, help me." She sat back down on the couch. "See, it's just that I don't know— Oh God—" She looked up at her brother. "Oh dear God please help me." She stood up again, shaking her hands furiously. "I don't know what to *do,* I don't know what to *do*—"

Vicky and Pete glanced at each other.

"I'm having a panic attack," Lucy said to them. "I haven't had one in ages, but this is a bad one, oh God, oh dear God. Oh Jesus, oh God— Okay, now listen to me, you guys, *listen* to me. Pete, can you drive my car, and, Vicky, I'll drive with you? Can you, please, oh, please can you, I have to—I just have to—"

"Drive you where?" Vicky asked.

"Chicago. The Drake Hotel. I have to get back, I just have to—"

"To *Chicago*?" Vicky asked. "You want me to drive you to Chicago? That's like two and a half hours away."

"Yes, can you do that? Oh God, I am so sorry, I am so sorry, I can't I can't I can't—"

Vicky looked at her wristwatch. She took a deep breath, widened her eyes for a moment. Then she turned and picked up her red pocketbook. "Let's go to Chicago," she said to Pete.

"Oh God, thank you, thank you—" Lucy was already opening the door.

Pete mouthed the words to Vicky: I've never been there. Vicky mouthed back: I know, but I have. Pointing to her chest.

※

In spite of the sun, the day was not hot. There was a clarity to the air that spoke of the autumn to come; Pete felt this as he got into Lucy's white rental car and waited while Vicky turned her car around; Lucy's car smelled new and was clean. Then he followed his sisters out to the main road. He could not believe he was to drive to Chicago. He sort of thought he might die. He drove along the narrow roads that were at first familiar, then he followed his sister's car to the highway. As the sun went slowly across the sky, he drove steadily behind his sister; more than an hour passed by. He could see them, Vicky, her shoulders broad, every so often turning to look at Lucy, who, her head lower, sat in the passenger seat. He drove and drove. He drove past oak trees and maple trees, he drove past big barns with American flags painted on their sides, he drove past a sign that said FIREARMS AND MEMORIES; he drove past an enormous place filled with John Deere trucks and machines, he drove past a sign that said ONE DAY DENTURES $144, he drove by an old shopping mall, no longer in use, that had grass growing up through the cement parking lot. On the steering wheel, his palms were sweating. There was a lot more time to go.

But his sister's car was suddenly blinking its light, slowing down, and Vicky pulled the car over into the breakdown lane. Pete had to step on the brakes quickly, and even then he went past his sister, but he pulled the car over in front of her.

As he stepped out of the car a truck went by him so quickly that a storm of air blasted over him. Lucy was getting out of the passenger side of Vicky's car, and she ran up to him. "I'm okay, Pete," she said; her eyes seemed smaller to him. She threw her arms around him briefly, and her head bumped his chin. "Thank you with all my heart," she said. "Now you go, I can drive myself into the city."

"You sure?" He felt confusion and some terror as another truck went by so fast, so close. "Lucy, be careful."

Lucy said, "I love you, Pete," and then she was gone, getting into her white rental car, and he waited while he saw her adjust the seat up. She stuck her head out of the open window. "Go, go," she shouted, waving her arm. Then she shouted something else, and Pete walked partway back to her. "Tell Vicky to remember about Anna-Marie, tell her, Pete!"

So he waved at her, and then turned back and got into Vicky's car, the seat slightly warm from where Lucy had been sitting. On the floor were empty soda cans, and he had to move his feet around them. Pete and Vicky followed Lucy until they came to the next exit, then they turned off to head back. In Pete's mind was the image of Lucy's white car going down the highway into the city. He felt stunned.

In a few minutes, when they were headed back on the right road, Vicky said, "Okay. Well, here's the story." She glanced over at Pete as she drove. "Lucy is coo-coo."

"Seriously?"

"She's completely coo-coo. She kept crying and saying, I'm sorry, I'm sorry, and I finally said, Lucy, stop being sorry, it's okay. And she kept saying, No, it was wrong of me to come, it was wrong of me to leave, it was all wrong of me, and I said, Lucy, stop this right now. You got the hell out, and you've made a life, stay out, it's *okay*. She wouldn't stop crying, Pete. It was a little scary. I said, Why don't you give your husband a call? And she said he was at rehearsal or something and she'd speak to him later, and I said, Well, try one of your girls, and she said, Oh no, she couldn't let her girls hear her like this."

Pete stared at the glove compartment; there were streaks down it, like coffee had been spilled there long ago. "Wow," he said. "I don't know what to say."

"Nothing." Vicky passed a car, pulled back in to the lane. "Anyway, she took a pill, and then said how panic attacks were— I can't remember what she said, but she calmed down and made me pull over so we wouldn't have to drive into the city. But, Pete, that was *sad*. She's so small, and she's— You see her online and—" Vicky fell silent. She sat up straighter and drove with one hand; the other hand was touching her chin; her elbow was on the armrest next to her. They drove along for quite a while.

Finally Vicky said, looking straight ahead at the road, "She's not coo-coo, Pete. She just couldn't stand being back here. It was too hard for her."

On his trips to the soup kitchen in Carlisle with the Guptills, Pete had noticed how they were affectionate toward each other; Shirley would often put her hand on Tommy's arm as he drove the car. Pete wondered about this, what it would be like to be that free, to touch people so freely. He would have liked—only not really—to put his own hand on his sister's arm right now, this sister who had put on lipstick to see the famous Lucy. Instead he sat quietly next to her.

Eventually Vicky said, "I never should have mentioned that stuff from the past."

"No, Vicky. How would you know? And I said the stuff about the clothes."

As they drove, the sun was glaring to their side. They passed once again the barns with the American flags painted on them, only they were on the other side of them now, and Pete saw once again, from across the road, the huge John Deere place with all its green and yellow machines. He felt awfully safe sitting next to Vicky. He kept wondering how he could tell her this, and he finally said, "Vicky, you're great."

She made a sound of disgust and glanced at him, and he said, "No, really, you are. Lucy said to remind you of the Anne-Marie woman."

"*Anna*-Marie." Then Vicky said, "What did she mean by that?"

"I think she meant that you were great too, that's what I think she was saying." Pete moved his feet around the cans that were on the floor there.

They drove in silence for many miles. From the corner of his eye, he watched his sister; he thought she was a good driver. He liked her bulkiness, the way she filled her seat and drove with such authority. He wished he could tell her this; he wished he could say something more than that she was great. He finally said, "Vicky, we didn't turn out so bad, you know."

She glanced at him and rolled her eyes. "Yeah, right," she said. Then she said, "Well, we're not out there murdering people, if that's what you mean." She gave a brief laugh that seemed to rise up from the deepest part of herself.

Pete wished the ride could go on forever. He wished he could sit there next to his sister while they drove and drove.

But he recognized where they were now; the roads were narrowing. He saw the top of a maple tree that had started to turn pink; he saw the fields that surrounded the Pedersons' barn. And then finally they were back; Vicky pulled in to the road, and then the driveway, and there in front of them was the tired little house with its blinds open. Vicky turned the car off. After a moment, Pete said, "Hey, Vicky, do you want that rug?"

Vicky pushed her glasses up her nose with a finger placed in the middle of them. "Sure, why not?" she said. But she made no move to get out of the car, and so they gazed at the house, in silence, and sat.

Dottie's Bed & Breakfast

They were from the East, and their name was Small.

This Dottie always remembered, because the husband was so big, and he wore a look of fixed irritation that must have come, at least partly, Dottie imagined, from a lifetime of responding to comments regarding his name. Which of course Dottie took no part in—not one bit!—at all. Mrs. Small had made the reservation over the telephone, so Dottie knew they weren't young. Not only Mrs. Small's voice told her this, but most people did things online now. Dottie was, in fact, a bit older than Mrs. Small, but Dottie had taken to the Internet like a paddlefish waiting for water; she was sorry it hadn't arrived when she was a younger woman, she was certain she could have been successful at something that made use of her mind more than the renting out of rooms for these past many years. She could have been rich! But Dottie was not a woman to complain, having been taught by her decent Aunt Edna one summer—it seemed like a hundred years ago, and practically was—that a complaining woman was like pushing dirt beneath the fingernails of God, and this was an image Dottie had never been able to fully dislodge. Dottie was a tiny woman, prim, with the good skin of her Midwestern ancestors, and all things considered—and there were many things to consider—she appeared—to herself and to others—to do just fine. In the event, the reservation was made for Mr. and Mrs. Small, and two weeks later a tall—big—white-haired man stepped through the door and said, "We have a reservation for Dr. Richard Small." Dr. Small's announcement was apparently large enough to include his wife, who came in right behind him, without any mention of her at all.

Standing at the front desk, he did the registering with terrible penmanship, irritation oozing out of him, while Mrs. Small—who was very thin and had a look of general nervousness about her—glanced politely around the lounge, and then became interested in the old photographs of the theater that were on the wall, and she seemed to especially like a photograph of the library that was hanging near them. The photo showed the library back in 1940 looking brick-and-ivy old-fashioned, so Dottie had a sense about this woman—and her husband!—right away. Of course, in Dottie's business she would have a sense about people right away. Sometimes of course Dottie had been very wrong. With the Smalls she was not wrong: Dr. Small complained immediately about the room having no luggage rack for him to place his suitcase on, and naturally Dottie did not say that's what happens when you have your wife call and ask for the cheapest room. Instead she said she had another room at the end of the hall that might serve them better; it was the Bunny Rabbit Room—that's what she called it due to the fact that in the past she'd had a habit of collecting stuffed toy bunnies. Her husband had given her one each holiday, and friends had too, so later Dottie put them all in one room, and, really, people went crazy for them sometimes. Women did. And gay men. They got quite imaginative with all those bunnies around, having them talking in different voices and so forth. Dottie used to have a Comment Book until people wrote things about seeing ghosts in the Bunny Rabbit Room and other foolishness. But the Bunny Rabbit Room had two beds and a low chest on which Dr. Small could place his suitcase, and that evening Dottie heard through the walls a constant thin-voiced monologue coming from Mrs. Small, with only once or twice a short answer from her husband. Dottie could not make out many words, but she understood that he was here for the cardiology convention and was not staying in the large hotel in town where the meeting was taking place, most likely, Dottie thought, because he was getting old and was no longer really respected. And he could not stand that, could not put up with seeing younger colleagues laughing together in the evenings, and so he had come here, to Dottie's Bed & Breakfast, where he could be not noticeably unimportant. "A physician," she imagined him saying at breakfast, because this is what all male doctors said when they didn't want you to think they were academics, to whom, Dottie had come to understand, physicians seemed to feel very superior. Dottie didn't care one way or another, anymore, whom anyone felt superior to, but in this business you did notice things; even if you kept your eyes squeezed shut, you would still notice things in this business. And the time of Dr. Small, Dottie thought, his own personal history in time, his own career, had passed, and he couldn't stand it. She was sure he made huge fusses about computerized records, the cost of the practice, the fact that he no longer made as much money. Well, she did not feel sorry for him.

But his wife surprised her.

When Dottie saw couples like Mr. and Mrs. Small, she was sometimes comforted that her painful divorce years earlier had at least prevented her from becoming a Mrs. Small—in other words, a nervous, slightly whiny woman whose husband ignored her and so naturally made her more anxious. This you saw all the time. And when Dottie saw it, she was reminded that almost always—oddly, she thought it was odd—she seemed a stronger person without her husband, even though she missed him every day.

But in fact, Mrs. Small, during breakfast—her husband was not talking to her but instead looking through a binder that perhaps contained his materials for the day—broke into song. She had been glancing through a stack of old theater programs Dottie kept in a basket, and while she was waiting for her toast she called out, "Oh, I love that Gilbert and Sullivan," and she started singing a chorus from *H.M.S. Pinafore*—with two other guests sitting a table away. Dottie thought Dr. Small would stop her, but he sang a few bars with her and that warmed Dottie's heart. It did, though she was always nervous, naturally, about the comfort of other guests, but the others didn't seem to mind, or even really to notice, people being, as Dottie knew, mostly very involved with themselves.

Oatmeal for Dr. Small and whole wheat toast for his wife—who Dottie noticed was wearing all black—and in a few minutes his wife said, "Richard, look. Annie Appleby! Look, it says right here, she was Martha Cratchit in *A Christmas Carol*, eight years ago. Look." She gave the program a little punch with her finger, then he took the program from her.

"Everything all right then?" Dottie asked, placing the food on the table. Almost in a British way, she liked to say that, though Dottie had never been to England in her life.

Mrs. Small's eyes were shiny as she turned to Dottie. "Annie Appleby used to be a friend of ours. Well, she was someone we knew. She was someone we—" Her husband cut her off with a subtle gesture of the sort that long-married couples can use with each other, and they finished their breakfast in silence.

Midmorning they left the house together. They left the house, which is what everyone who came there did: leave. Dottie was always reminded that people were there to visit others, or—as in the case of the Smalls—to be part of their business world, or, frequently, to see their children at the college. Whatever it was, they were connected to something in the little city of Jennisberg, Illinois; they stepped out into the street with a purpose. The big oak door closing, accentuating this, the muffling of voices the moment they were on the front porch, the inescapable whisper of abandonment—well, that was part of the business too.

⁜

Mrs. Small came back alone right after lunch. She undid the scarf from around her neck and dallied a bit in the lounge, looking at the old photos on the wall, while Dottie worked behind the desk. "I'm Shelly," said Mrs. Small. "I don't know if I properly introduced myself before." Dottie said it was lovely having her stay, and continued with her business. People sometimes got confused in a B&B, not knowing how friendly they should be, and Dottie understood this; she tried to give allowances. In Dottie's youth she had been extremely poor, and for many years afterward—more than needed to be—whenever she went into a store, whether a dress shop or the butcher's or a pastry shop or a department store, she expected to be watched and then asked to leave. Dottie held this indignity dear; anyone who came into her B&B was never to feel that way. And Shelly Small, who gave no indication of having suffered poverty of any kind— though of course one never knew—was really very nervous; Dottie was aware of that. In a few minutes Shelly brought up the actress Annie Appleby again. As she stood looking at the photo of the theater, Shelly said to Dottie, but without looking at Dottie, "I think about Annie a lot. Much more than I need to, let's just say that." She gave Dottie a quick smile then, and what passed over her face was a look that caused Dottie to feel for a moment as if a small fish had swum through her stomach, a feeling she recognized as a symptom of—well, almost pity, though pity was a confusing thing, and Dottie would hate for people to pity her, as she knew had been done in the past.

Dottie suddenly asked the woman if she would like a cup of tea, and Shelly said, "Oh, wouldn't that be nice," and so they sat in the living room, which was really the lounge. Shelly Small didn't take more than one sip of the tea; that was just a prop, as they would say in the world of theater, just a piece of furniture, so to speak, allowing her to sit in Dottie's house on that autumn day while the light shifted through the room. That cup of tea, Dottie saw, gave her permission to talk.

And to the best of Dottie's ability, as she recalled it later, this was the gist of what Shelly said:

Dr. Small had served in Vietnam years ago with another physician, a man named David Sewall. They were never in danger in Vietnam, Shelly claimed; it was quite dull, really. They worked in a hospital in a safe area toward the end of the war, with plenty of notice to leave the country in time,

they were not hanging from helicopters during the fall of
Saigon, nothing like that, nor did they, in the hospital, even
see a lot of "awful stuff," really—Shelly didn't want Dottie
to get the impression that these men were traumatized the
way so many people were . . . Well, you know, those who
served— Okay. Slapping her hands gently down onto her
black-slacked thighs. So. When Richard came home from
the war he met Shelly on a train that was heading to Boston, and after a year they got married and David was their
best man. David later became a psychiatrist and married a
very pretty woman named Isa. They had three sons. The
Small family and the Sewall family were friends—they lived
in the same town outside of Boston, and were both involved
with fundraising for the orchestra and, oh, you know how
things are, you get a set of friends and the Sewalls were
their friends. The wife, Isa, was always a little odd, un-
knowable, very restrained, but a nice woman. David drank
too much, everyone knew that, but he managed not to show
up at the office with drink on his breath, being a doctor or
a minister, those were the two professions where you could
never have drink on your breath—and the sons, oh, it didn't
matter, they were how sons are, two turned out fine, one
not so fine. Isa was always worried, David was often strict,
and the point is that after thirty years of marriage David
and Isa divorced. It shocked everyone. There were other
couples you'd have placed money on way before you'd have
placed any money on the Sewalls splitting up, but there you
are. Shelly Small raised her thin wrists, palms upward, and

gave a tiny shrug that was somehow very serious. "We had our own troubles, you know," she said. "For years I kept the name of a divorce lawyer in my desk drawer. Right up until we renovated the cottage on the lake for what will be our retirement home," she said. Dottie nodded her head just once.

It was Isa who had done the splitting, finding some man in a painting class that David, ironically, had pestered her to sign up for because he thought she was getting depressed, and David was livid, absolutely went to pieces. There were times he came to the Smalls' house and just wept, and Shelly had a hard time seeing that, to be honest. It was probably very old-fashioned of her, but she did not like to see a grown man cry. Richard was good—it irritated him, he found it tiresome, but he took it in stride, as any good friend would do.

And then after a couple of years of different women that David brought around, oh, Shelly wasn't going to go into them because they weren't the point. The point was Annie. Annie Appleby. Here Shelly sat up straighter, bent slightly toward Dottie, and said, "She was really special."

Dottie did not find it hard to listen to this.

"The thing about Annie—well, first you must realize she is very tall. About six feet, and she's thin, so she seems really tall, and she has long, dark, wavy, almost corkscrew hair—honestly I often wondered if there wasn't something else mixed in there, you know, maybe something else, along with some North American Indian. She comes from Maine.

Her face was lovely, lovely, the finest features and blue eyes, and—oh, how can I say this? She just made you happy. She loved everything. And when David first brought her around—"

Dottie asked how they had met.

Shelly's cheeks flushed red. "Richard would kill me for telling you, but she was a patient of David's. Well, he could have lost his license, but he did it the right way. He said he couldn't be her psychiatrist anymore— Look, the point is this happens sometimes, and it happened with them, and he brought her around—though it had to be a real secret, of course, how they met, they made up a story that her mother had known him in college, which was absolute nonsense. Annie was from a potato farm in Maine, for heaven's sake. But she'd been an actress since she was sixteen, just left home, apparently no one cared, and even if she was twenty-seven years younger than David, it didn't seem to make a bit of difference, they were happy. You just loved being around them."

Shelly paused and chewed on her lip. Her hair, which was the pale strawberry blond of someone who had once been a redhead, was thinning the way older women's hair is apt to do, and she had it cut—"appropriately" is the word that came into Dottie's mind—right above her chin; there was probably nothing very daring about Shelly, there probably never had been.

"You know," she said, "Richard was not sure he wanted to move to the lake."

Dottie raised her eyebrows, although she did think that Easterners tended to go on without the need of encouragement; this would not be the case with anyone from the Midwest. Incontinence was not valued in the Midwest.

"But that's a different story," Shelly said. "Well, sort of," she said.

For no reason she could think of, and it may have been nothing more than the way the sun was slanting right then across the hardwood floor, Dottie was suddenly visited by the memory of one summer of her childhood when she was sent to Hannibal, Missouri, to spend a number of weeks with an ancient and unfamiliar relative. She went alone—her beloved older brother, Abel, had secured a job in the local theater as an usher and therefore stayed at home—and Dottie was terrified; in the way of some children who are accustomed to deprivation, she understood little and did as she was told. Why her decent Aunt Edna could not take her, as she had done before, to this day Dottie did not know. The only memory she brought back was that of an article she read in a *Reader's Digest* stacked among meaningless magazines on a dusty windowsill, offering up the tale of a woman whose husband had served in Korea. At home with small children at the time, this wife—the woman who wrote the article—lived in the United States somewhere and raised the children and waited for each letter from her husband. He finally returned and there was much rejoicing. And then one day, about a year later, while her husband was at work and the children were at school, a knock came at the door. A small Korean woman stood there with a baby in her arms. Dottie was just at the age when she read this that her heart, so naïve in spite of what she had already learned about life, or rather what she had already absorbed about life, because people absorb first and learn later, if they learn at all, Dottie had been, at the time she read this article, at the age where her heart almost came through her throat as she imagined the woman who opened the door. The husband confessed: He was very sorry for all the disturbance, and it was decided he would divorce his steadfast wife and marry the Korean woman and raise the baby with her, and the steadfast wife, while brokenhearted, helped out, meaning, she allowed her children to visit her husband's new home, and she gave advice to the young woman, got her into an English class, and when the husband suddenly died, the first wife took in the young woman and her child and helped them get onto their feet until they could move somewhere else and get settled, and even then, at the time she was writing the article, she was helping to put the child through college, a truly Christian story if there ever was one. All this had made a rather significant impact on Dottie. She wept silently and fulsomely, young girl tears rolling down her cheeks, dropping onto the pages; the woman, betrayed and largehearted, became a heroine to Dottie. The woman forgave everybody.

When it came time for Dottie's own knock on the door,

she naturally remembered this story. She came to understand that people had to decide, really, how they were going to live.

✳

Shelly Small sat in the armchair looking at the floor with an expression of misery, and Dottie said, "Where is the house, Shelly?"

"On a lake in New Hampshire." Shelly sat up straighter, revived. "We bought it years ago as a small cottage, a darling little place, and we'd go up there weekends and in the summer for most of August if we could, and I loved it. I loved watching the water change with the sky, and in April there would be flowering laurel trees, just beautiful. I wanted us to retire there."

"And why not?" Dottie said.

"I'll tell you why not. Richard was not for it. And as time went on"—Shelly leaned forward in her chair—"as time went on, you see— Well, I'll just say this, being a doctor's wife is not a bowl of cherries. Doctors think they're terribly important, honestly. And I raised the children and he would tell me I wasn't doing it right, but was he there when the school called to say that Charlotte had just been caught defacing the girls' room in the most disgusting way? No, of course not." She suddenly laughed. "Well, finally for the first time in our marriage I put my foot down and I said, If you are not going to join me in rebuilding this cottage into a retirement home for us, then you are not the man I thought you were and not the man for me." She waved a thin arm. "That's all water under the bridge. I designed a lovely house, all that was required by the zoning laws was to keep the original footprint of the house, you know, just do that, keep the *original footprint,* and I brought in some architects from Boston and it took almost two years, but there it is, a lovely house, we were able to build it up high—it's four floors, you know—and also down, by digging out a bit of the ground, so really it's four and a half stories, it's a lovely house. And we have friends come up on weekends, and we'll retire there. Very soon. Richard's tired of the way things are going. No one can really make a living in medicine anymore."

"Get back to the Annie girl," Dottie said.

Shelly's face took on a quickness of expression. "She was hardly a girl. But she did seem it. She did seem like a girl." And Shelly talked on quietly and steadily. It was getting dark by the time the door opened and her husband came in, and Dottie could see immediately how dismissive he was of his wife and the B&B proprietor sitting in the living room chatting over cold undrunk cups of tea. He spoke briefly, then went straight to their room, and Shelly, with a rather furtive and quick smile toward Dottie, gathered her things and followed.

✳

Annie Appleby was much as Shelly had described her: Dottie found interviews and reviews and blogs and of course photographs, and the girl was really exceptional. She did not have that open-faced shiny thing that actresses so often had, as though they wanted to beam their way right out of the photo and into your lap. Very childlike, Dottie thought actors were, from what she saw on TV when they had their silly interviews, and on the Web too, but Annie didn't look like that. She looked like you could stare at her forever and not know something you wanted to know that she was not going to let you know. It was a very attractive quality; Dottie could see a psychiatrist having trouble with the likes of her each week staring at him across the room, or lying down, or whatever it was a patient going to a psychiatrist did. Annie seemed to have stopped being an actress for quite a while, though. Dottie couldn't find anything about what she was up to now.

✳

Shelly had said that she and Annie had walked around the lake the last time Annie and David had visited, which was the first time Annie and David had seen the new house. The new house had a visitors' suite downstairs where Annie and David had right away taken their bags, and Annie had said, Oh, how beautiful, Shelly, what an amazing job you've done! So then they had taken a walk around the lake, the men walking ahead of the women, and Shelly told Annie things. Of course Dottie wondered: What things? And of course Shelly told her without being asked. "What I told Annie was that I was older now, and it made life different. I mean," Shelly said, straightening the top of her trousers, "Annie had this quality that made you feel you could really talk to her, and so that last day, that last time they were at the lake, I told her how I remembered years ago, when I was a young girl, a man passed me in the concert hall and said, Well, you're a pretty thing, and I told Annie this. And I said, No one will ever tell me I'm pretty again."

Dottie had to allow a minute for this to sink in. "And what did she say?" Dottie asked.

Shelly cocked her head. "I don't really remember. She had the gift of not saying much, just listening, and you thought it was all going to be okay."

Dottie thought that Shelly had put Annie in quite a tight spot that day, saying no one would ever again tell her she was pretty. Shelly Small did not have the remnants of pretty on her. Perhaps she had once had the remnants of pretty, but Dottie could not see it.

"And I told her other things," Shelly said. "I told her how worried I was about my children's marriages. My younger daughter, well, she'd become quite . . . overweight, and I really didn't understand it. And just the weekend before they had been at the lake and I'd watched while her husband encouraged her to eat more. I told Annie all about it. I said, Why would he do that? And Annie said she didn't know. And I told her how my other daughter was just desperate for a different job— Well, I told her private things."

"Yes, I see," said Dottie.

"But here's the thing—" Shelly pressed her legs together and leaned forward, her hands held together in her thin lap. "After Annie and David broke up, I called Annie and said she could come to the lake herself, we'd be happy to have her anytime, I left a message, and she never called back. Never called me back. And so when David arrived in one of his weeping states—just weeping away, like he did after Isa left him—I told him this, that Annie had never called me back, and he said, 'Of course she didn't call you back, Shelly. Annie thought you were pathetic! She thought you were an idiot!' "

She didn't think that, Shelly had answered, and even Richard told David to go easy. "She did," said David. So Shelly, of course shaken, said, Oh, David, the whole thing was a little unrealistic anyway, you know. Just with the age difference alone. And David said, staring out at the water, "The age difference. Here's what I have learned about the age difference. People think girls like older men because they want a father. Classic theory. But girls want older men so they can boss them around. They're wearing the pants, I can tell you that. She was nothing but a whore."

This made Shelly very uncomfortable, and she told the men she was going to start dinner, and then she hesitated and said, David, I put your stuff downstairs in the guest suite, but maybe you don't want to stay there because, you know—that's where—

"That's where nothing," David said. "That's where Annie recoiled from me and said she hated this huge new house. She said, 'This house is Shelly's penis.' That's what she said."

Here Shelly stopped telling the story. Unmistakably, tears popped into her eyes.

Dottie wanted to laugh out loud. Oh, she really did. Dottie thought it was one of the funniest things she'd heard in a very long time. And then she glanced up at Shelly and saw that in spite of what Dottie always thought was a placid front that she—Dottie—presented to the world, Shelly Small had felt Dottie's desire to laugh, and she was furious. Well, she would be furious, Dottie understood. After all, the point of the woman's story was that Annie had humiliated her. Humiliation is not to be laughed at; Dottie knew that well.

Still.

Dottie arranged the crocheted doily that covered the armrest of the chair she sat in. She was aware within herself of some contest of feeling. She felt for Shelly. And yet Dottie could tell by the light that had passed through the room that Shelly must have been talking for almost two hours. About herself. Oh, about Annie and David and her daughters, but really she was talking about herself. Had Dottie talked about herself for so long, she'd have felt that she had wet herself. This was a matter of different cultures, Dottie knew that, although she felt it had taken her many years to learn this. She thought that this matter of different cultures was a fact that got lost in the country these days. And culture included class, which of course nobody ever talked about in this country, because it wasn't polite, but Dottie also thought people didn't talk about class because they didn't really understand what it was. For example, had people known that Dottie and her brother had eaten from dumpsters when they were children, what would they make of it? Her brother for years now had lived in a huge expensive house outside of Chicago and ran an air-conditioning company, and Dottie was trim and neat, and really quite caught up on world events, and ran this B&B very effectively, so what would people say? That she and her brother, Abel, were the American Dream, and that the rest who still ate from dumpsters deserved to do so? A lot of people would secretly feel this way. Shelly Small with her big husband and thinning hair might very well feel this way.

Shelly Small had been raised to speak about herself as though she was the most interesting thing in the world. Listening to her, Dottie almost admired this. Because even having—perhaps—caught Dottie's desire to laugh, Shelly could not be stopped. She was speaking now of the people in this town where their lake house was, how these people had been pleasant and welcoming before the renovation. Now neighbors drove by without even waving. One had stopped, rolled down his window, and accused her of spoiling the lakefront with a McMansion. "Oh, honestly," Shelly said. "Imagine such foolishness. We kept the original footprint!"

Dottie stood up and walked to her desk, pretending that something there required her attention, all this to avoid having Shelly see her face. "Sorry, but if I don't put this bill on the top of my papers it won't get paid." Dottie rustled some papers and added, "I don't believe Annie said any of those things about you. She doesn't sound like a person who would say that—at all."

"But of course she said it!" Shelly wailed from her chair in the living room.

"That your house was your penis?" Dottie didn't often say the word "penis," and she enjoyed it. She came back around from behind her desk and returned to sit near Shelly again. "Does that really sound like what this Annie would say? 'David, this house is Shelly's penis.'"

Shelly Small's cheeks were quite red. "I don't know."

"Well, true enough," Dottie agreed. "You don't. But I think—if you really *think* about it—well, isn't saying that the house was your penis something a psychiatrist would say? Think about it, Mrs. Small. Who thinks in those terms? Why, my friends and I might say things about other people we know, but we don't go around saying their house is their penis. Look at this house. This is my house. Would you say to Mr. Small—would you say to Dr. Small tonight, this house, this bed-and-breakfast, is that woman's penis?"

And right then the door opened and Dr. Small walked in

with all the breezes of an Illinois autumn surrounding him. "How are you, ladies?" he asked, unbuttoning his coat. "Shelly?" As though the poor wife should not sit and chat with a B&B proprietor. And off she followed him to their room.

*

What Dottie had not understood until the Smalls came to stay was that there were different experiences she attended to in this business that made her feel either connected to or used by other people. For example, there had been the dear, dear man who came in one night about dinnertime—a man almost but not quite her age—and took his room and then decided he'd rather watch television, and she'd sat with him watching one of those British comedies—oh, Dottie thought they were funny, and she tried not to laugh out loud since this man was not laughing—when she became aware that he was in serious distress. He began to make a noise that she had never heard before; it was not entirely unsexual in its sound, but it was a sound of terrible pain. Unspeakable pain, she often thought later. He mimed to her, as she quietly asked questions, and Dottie found it re-markable how much they were able to understand each other. First thing, she'd asked if he needed a doctor, and he shook his head and waved a hand in a way that indicated this was nothing a doctor could help with. Tears began slipping sloppily down the man's deeply creased face; oh, bless his poor soul, she always thought, remembering him. Okay, she had said, and she sat on the couch next to him, and he looked at her so searchingly, so deeply, she had never been looked at by any man so deeply, she thought, or looked at a man that deeply herself, and he was positively mute, even though earlier, asking for a room and then permission to watch television, he had most certainly been able to use words. She stayed calm and made statements he could either agree with by nodding or disagree with by a dismal shake of his head. For example, she said: "I'm going to stay right here to make sure you're all right." And he nodded, those poor tired eyes searching hers. She said: "Something seems to have happened to you, but you will be okay, I think." She said: "I'm not frightened by this, just so you know." And that caused a sudden extra burst of effluvia from his eyes, and he squeezed her hand hard enough to almost break it. Then he held up the same hand in what Dottie took to be a gesture of apology. She said: "No worries, I know you meant no harm." He shook his head sadly in agreement. Dottie could no longer recall every part of this, but the two of them did, it seemed to her, communicate quite well, all things considered—and apparently there were many things to consider!—and she was able, by asking, to find out that at midnight he could take a pill and sleep for five hours. "All righty," she said. "But not too many pills, am I correct?" He had nodded. And in this way—really, it was a remarkable event—they had spent the evening together while he seemed to wash out his very soul in front of her. At midnight she brought him water and walked him to his room and told him where her room was should he need her, and then she had raised an index finger and said, "Not an invitation, which I'm sure you understand, but I always feel it's best to be clear about things," and he had almost laughed, with real mirth, she could see his eyes relax, and they had this sort of not-out-loud but quite riotous laughter about what she had said. He left at seven in the morning: a tall man, and not altogether badlooking now that his face was washed by rest, and he had said "I thank you very much" with embarrassment and sincerity. She did not ask if he needed breakfast, she understood the awkwardness of his being served eggs and toast by a woman who had seen something she had not been meant to see, that no one had been meant to see.

And so he left. They always did leave.

She kept his registration form the way a child would keep a ticket stub as a souvenir of a special day. Honest as a brook in spring, the entire thing had been. She never looked him up on the Internet, nor was she ever tempted. Charlie Macauley was his name. Charlie Macauley of the unspeakable pain.

✳

The next morning at breakfast Shelly did not acknowledge Dottie. Not even a thank you for the whole wheat toast. Dottie was very surprised; her eyes watered with the sudden sting of this. But then she understood. There was an old African proverb Dottie had read one day that said, "After a man eats, he becomes shy." And Dottie thought of that now with Shelly. Shelly was like the man in the proverb; having satisfied her needs, she was ashamed. She had confided more than she had wanted to, and now Dottie was somehow to blame. As Dottie thought about this, going back and forth between the kitchen and the dining room, she saw Shelly Small as a woman who suffered only from the most common complaint of all: Life had simply not been what she thought it would be. Shelly had taken life's disappointments and turned them into a house. A house that, with the clever use of the right architects, had managed to stay within the legal code yet became a monstrosity as large as Shelly's needs. Tears had not popped into her eyes over her daughter's obesity. No, they came to her when she reported the assault upon her vanity. She had won against her husband the War of the House, but it had not been enough. What Dottie had not said to her, because it was not her place, was that Shelly had a husband who would break into song at the breakfast table with her in a room with strangers sitting nearby, and that was no— excuse me, Dottie thought—small thing.

To listen to a person is not passive. To really listen is active, and Dottie had really listened. And Dottie thought that Shelly's problems, her humiliations, were not large when you considered what was happening in the world. When you considered the people dying of starvation, get-

ting blown up for no reason, being gassed by their own government, you choose it—this was not the story of Shelly
Small. And yet Dottie had felt for her small—yes, Small—
moments of human sadness. And now Shelly could not return the decency of even looking her in the eye. This kind
of thing Dottie did not care for, she would like to know
who would!

When Shelly did glance over her shoulder to inquire
whether there was more jam to be had, Dottie said there
was, of course. In the kitchen—and while it was a terribly
conventional form of revenge—she spit in the jam and
mixed it up and spit again, as much as she could gather in
her mouth, and took some pleasure in seeing the jam bowl
empty by the time the Smalls left. People had been spitting
in the food of those they served most likely since the beginning of time. Dottie knew from experience that the ease
this provided was very short-lived, but then most ease was
short-lived, and that is how life was.

Shelly was out for the entire day, and the couple did not
return to their room until very late. That night Dottie
heard—and she was surprised—so much suppressed gig-
gling coming from the Bunny Rabbit Room that she got out
of bed and walked in her slippers down the hall. And what
she heard was Shelly Small making fun of Dottie in terms
Dottie found outrageous. These terms had to do with Dottie's body parts ostensibly not having been made use of in
quite some time, and Dr. Small, not surprisingly, was quite
graphic during his part of the discussion and they had a

very merry time doing this, as though Dottie was a clown
on stage tripping over shoes too large; their humor was like
that. And then began, as Dottie realized would happen, the
sounds of people, as her decent Aunt Edna had put it, who
love each other. Only Dottie did not hear the sounds of
love—she heard sounds from the man that made her think
how some women thought of men as pigs. Dottie had never
thought of men as pigs, but this man did a good imitation;
it was revolting—and intriguing—in the most ghastly way.
Listening in the hallway, she did not hear the sounds of a
woman enjoying the love of her husband. Instead she heard
the sounds of a woman who would do anything to make
herself feel superior to an old lady who was, as Shelly had
put it only minutes earlier, so puritanical as to object to almost anything. In other words, the unhappiness of Shelly
Small was something she could ease by being a sexual
woman, unlike Dottie. But she was not a sexual woman,
Dottie could tell. Shelly got into the shower promptly after,
and to Dottie this was always the sign of a woman who had
not enjoyed her man.

In the morning only Dr. Small was at the breakfast table.
"And will your wife be joining you?" Dottie asked.
    "She is packing," he said, unfolding his napkin. "I'll
have the oatmeal again, and you needn't prepare anything
for her."

Dottie nodded, and after bringing him his oatmeal she
went to help check out the other couple that had been staying there as well. When she returned to the dining room Dr.
Small was just standing up, throwing his napkin onto his
oatmeal bowl. Dottie felt a deep sense of revulsion—she
had been used.

Placing her hands on the top of a dining room chair, she
said calmly, "I am not a prostitute, Dr. Small. That is not
my profession, you see."

Unlike his wife, who turned red quickly when surprised
or embarrassed, this man turned pale, and Dottie knew—
because Dottie knew many things—that this was a far
worse sign.

"What in the world do you mean by that?" he finally
said. He seemed unable to help but add "Jesus *Christ,* lady."

Dottie stayed exactly where she was. "Precisely what I
said is what I mean. I offer guests a bed, and I offer them
breakfast. I do not offer them counsel from lives they find
unendurable." She closed her eyes briefly, then continued,
"Or from marriages that are living deaths, from disappointments suffered at the hands of poor friends who re-
gard their houses as a penis. This is not what I do."

"Jesus," said Dr. Small, who was backing away from her.
"You're a whackjob." He bumped into a chair, and seemed
almost ready to fall. He straightened himself and said,
pointing a finger, shaking it at her, "You shouldn't be dealing with the public, good Christ." He walked into the living

room, then headed up the stairs. "I'm surprised no one's reported you, though I suspect they have. I'll go online myself, by God."

Dottie cleared the dishes. Calmness had come to her quickly and quietly. No one had ever lodged a complaint against her. Nor would Dr. Small, who most likely could barely use the Internet; his materials, she remembered, had been in a binder his first morning at the breakfast table.

Dottie waited until she heard the Smalls descending the stairs. Then she went and held the front door open for them; she did not say "Fly safely," because she did not care if they flew right into the sea, but when she saw Shelly's red nose, the drop of fluid hanging from its tip, Dottie felt momentarily sad. But Dr. Small said, as he pushed past Dottie with his suitcase, "What a goddamn whackjob, Jesus Christ," and then Dottie felt the wonderful calmness come to her again. She said politely, "Goodbye now," and closed the door behind them.

Then she went and sat behind her desk. The house was absolutely silent. In a few minutes she saw the Smalls' rental car drive from the driveway, and then she took from the far back of her top drawer the slip of paper with the lovely man's name on it: Charlie Macauley. Charlie Macauley of the Unspeakable Pain. Dottie kissed two fingers and pressed them to his signature.

Snow-Blind

Back then the road they lived on was a dirt road and they lived at the end of it, about a mile from Route 4. This was in the north, in potato country, and back when the Appleby children were small, the winters were icy and snow-filled and there were months when the road seemed impassably narrow. Weather was different then, like a family member you couldn't avoid. You took it without thinking much. Elgin Appleby attached a sturdy snowplow to his sturdiest tractor, and he was usually able to clear the way enough to get the kids to school. Elgin had grown up in farm country and he knew about weather and he knew about potatoes and he knew who in the county sold their bags with hidden rocks for weight. He was a closed book of a man, he inhabited himself with economy, but his family understood that he loathed dishonesty in any form. He did have surprising and sudden moments of liveliness. For example, he could

imitate perfectly old Miss Lurvy, who ran the Historical Society's tiny museum—"The first flush toilet in Aroostook
County," he would say, heaving back his narrow shoulders
as though he had a large bosom, "belonged to a judge who
was known to beat his wife quite regularly." Or he might
pretend to be a tramp looking for food, holding out his
hand, his blue eyes beseeching, and his children would
laugh themselves sick, until his wife, Sylvia, got them
calmed down. On winter mornings he let the car warm up
in the driveway as he scraped the ice from its windows, ex-
haust billowing about him until the kids tumbled down the
salt-dappled snow on the steps. There were three other kids
on the road, the two boys in the Daigle family and their
sister, Charlene, who was close to the age of the youngest
Appleby child, a strange little girl named Annie.

Annie was skinny and lively and so prone to talkative-
ness that her mother was not altogether sorry when the
child spent hours by herself in the woods playing with
sticks or making angels in the snow. Annie was the only
Appleby child to inherit the Acadian olive skin tone and
dark hair from her mother and grandmother, and the sight
of her red hat and dark head coming across the snowfields
was as common as seeing a nuthatch at the birdfeeder. One
morning when Annie was five and going to kindergarten
she told the car full of children—her brother and sister and
the Daigle boys and Charlene—that God spoke to her when
she was outside in the woods. Her sister said, "You're so
stupid, why don't you shut up." Annie bounced on the seat

beside her father and she said, "He does, though! God talks to me." Her sister asked how did he do that, and Annie answered, "He puts thoughts in my head." Annie looked up at her father then, and saw something in his eyes as he turned to look at her that stayed with her always, something that did not seem like her father, not yet, something that seemed not good. "You all get out," he said when he pulled up in front of the school. "I have to speak to Annie." When the car doors had slammed shut he said to his daughter, "What is it you saw in the woods?"

She thought about this. "I saw the trees and chickadees."

Her father stayed silent a long time, gazing over the top of the steering wheel. Annie had never been scared of her father the way Charlene was scared of hers. And Annie wasn't scared of her mother, who was the cozier parent but not the more important one. "Go on now." Her father nodded at her, and she pushed herself across the seat, her snow pants squeaking, and he leaned and got the door, saying "Watch your fingers" before he pulled it shut.

※

That was the year Jamie did not like his teacher. "He makes me sick," Jamie said, throwing his boots into the mudroom. Like his father, Jamie was not a talker, and Sylvia, watching this, had a quick flush come to her face.

"Is Mr. Potter mean to you?"

"No."

"Then what?"

"I don't know."

Jamie was in the fourth grade, and Sylvia loved him more than she loved her daughters; it was that he caused an almost unbearable sweetness to spread through her. That he should suffer anything was intolerable. She loved Annie gently because the child was so strange and harmless. The middle child, Cindy, Sylvia loved with a mild generosity. Cindy was the dullest of the three and probably the most like her mother.

It was also the year Jamie saved up his money and gave his father a tape recorder for his birthday. This turned into a terrible moment because his father, after unwrapping the present with barely any rips to the wrapping paper, the way he always unwrapped things, said, "You're the one who wants a tape recorder, James. It's indecent to give someone a present you want yourself, though it happens all the time."

"Elgin," Sylvia murmured. It was true that Jamie had wanted a tape recorder, and his pale cheeks burned red. The tape recorder was put away on the top shelf of the coat closet.

Annie, talkative as she was, did not mention this to anyone, including her grandmother next door. Her grandmother's house was a small square house, and in the long white months of winter the house seemed stark and bare naked, the windows like eyes stuck open, looking toward the farm. The old woman was from the St. John Valley and was said to have been beautiful in her day. Annie's mother had once been beautiful too, photos showed that. Now the old woman was stick-thin, and tiny wrinkles covered her face. "I would like to die," she said languidly from where she lay on her couch. Annie sat cross-legged in the big chair nearby. Her grandmother drew in the air with her finger. "I would like to close my eyes right now and pass away." She lifted her head of white hair and looked over at Annie. "I'm blue," she added. She put her head back down.

"I'd miss you," said Annie. It was a Saturday and it had snowed all day, the flakes big and wet and thick, sticking to the lower windowpanes in curves.

"You wouldn't. You only come over here to get a piece of candy. You have a brother and a sister to talk to. I don't know why the three of you don't play together."

"We're not in the appetite." Annie had once asked her brother to play cards and he had said he was not in the appetite. She picked at a hole in her sock. "Our teacher says if you look at the fields right after it snows and the sun is shining hard you can get blind." Annie craned her neck to see out the window.

"Then don't look," her grandmother said.

❋

When Annie was in the fifth grade, she began staying at Charlene Daigle's house more. Annie was still lively and talked incessantly, but there had been an incident with the long-forgotten tape recorder—a secret she shared with

Jamie—and ever since the incident it was as though a skin was compressed round her own family: the farm, her quiet brother, her sulky sister, her smiling mother, who often said, "I feel sorry for the Daigles. He's always so grumpy and he yells at the kids. We're awfully lucky to have a happy family." All of it made Annie picture a sausage, and she had poked a small hole in the casing and was trying to squirm out. Mr. Daigle did not really yell at his kids; in fact, when Annie and Charlene took a bath he often came in to wash them with a washcloth. Annie's own father thought bodies were private and had recently become red-faced and yelled—yelled hard!—because Cindy had not wrapped her sanitary pad adequately with toilet paper before putting it in the garbage. He had made her come and get it and wrap it up more. It caused Annie to tremble inside; the skin of the sausage was shame. Her family was encased in shame. She felt this more than she thought it, the way children do. But she thought that when she was old enough for this awful thing to happen to her own body she would bury the things outside in the woods.

So she went to Charlene's house after school and they made large snowpeople that Mr. Daigle sprayed with the hose so they would turn icy and glasslike by the morning. When it was too cold to be outside, Annie and Charlene made up stories and acted them out. Annie's father, stopping by to get her, would stand with Mrs. Daigle and watch them. Mrs. Daigle wore red lipstick, there was something fierce about her; Elgin Appleby got a twinkle in his eye when he talked with her. It was not a look he got when he talked to his wife, and one Saturday afternoon Annie said quite suddenly, "This is a dumb play we made up. I want to go home." Walking back up the road to their house she still held her father's hand, as she had always done. Around them the fields were endless and white, edged by the dark trunks of spruce trees and their boughs weighed down with the snow. "Daddy," she said, blurting it out, "what's the most important thing to you?"

"You, of course." He did not break his stride. "My family." His answer was immediate and calm.

"And Mama?"

"The most important of all."

Joy spilled around Annie, and in her memory it stayed that way for years. The walk back up the road to her house, holding her father's hand, the fields quieting in their brightness, the trees darkening to a navy green, the milky sun that was the color of the snow. Once inside the house she knocked softly on the door of her brother's room. He was in high school, and small hairs were on his upper lip. She closed the door behind her and said, "Nana's just a mean old witch. Nobody likes her. Not one person."

Her brother kept looking at the comic book he held open. "I don't know what you're talking about," he said. But when Annie sighed and turned to go, he said, "Of course she's an old hag. And don't worry about her. You always exaggerate everything." He was quoting his mother, who said that Annie exaggerated things.

The farm had belonged to Sylvia's father. Elgin had lived three towns away, though he had originally come from Illinois; he had been raised in a trailer with a family that had no money, farm, or religion. He had worked on farms, though, and knew the business, and after he married Sylvia he took over the farm when his father-in-law died. At some point, before Annie's memory, the house for her grandmother had been built. Until then she had lived in the main house with the rest of the family.

"Listen to this," Jamie had said, coming to Annie one day before supper, and they went to the barn and huddled in the loft. "I hid it under Nana's couch before Ma came over." The tape recorder clicked and whirred. Then there was the clear voice of their grandmother saying to her daughter, "Sylvia, it gags me. I lie here and I want to vomit. But you've made your bed. So you lie in the bed you made, my dear." And there was the sound of their mother crying. There was some murmur of a question. Should she speak to the priest? Their grandmother said, "I'd be too embarrassed, if I were you."

※

It seemed to be forever, the white snow around them, her grandmother next door lying on her couch wanting to die, Annie still the one who chattered constantly. She was now an inch short of six feet and thin as a wire, her dark hair long and wavy. Her father found her one day behind the barn and he said, "I want you to stop going off into the woods the way you do. I don't know what you're up to there." Her amazement had more to do with the disgust and anger of his expression. She said she was up to nothing. "I'm not asking you, I'm telling you, Annie, you stop or I'll see to it you never leave this house." She opened her mouth to say, Are you crazy?, but the thought touched her mind that maybe he was, and this frightened her in a way she had not known a person could be frightened. "Okay," she said. But it turned out she could not stay away from the woods on days when the sun was bright. The physical world with its dappled light was her earliest friend, and it waited with its open-armed beauty to accept her sense of excitement that nothing else could bring. She learned the rhythms of those around her, where they would be and when, and she slipped into the woods closer to town, or behind the school, and there she would sing with gentleness and exuberance a song she'd made up years earlier, "I'm so glad that I'm living, just so glaaad that I'm living—" She was waiting.

And then she wasn't waiting, because Mr. Potter saw her in a school play and arranged for her to be in a summer theater, and people in the summer theater took her to Boston, then she was gone. She was sixteen years old, and that her parents did not object, did not even ask her to finish high school, occurred to her only later. At the time there were various men, many of them fat and soft and with large rings on their fingers, who held her close in darkened theaters and murmured how lovely she was, like a fawn in the woods, and they sent her to different auditions, found her people to stay with in different rooms in different towns, people, she found, who were extraordinarily, unbelievably kind. The same compression of God's presence she knew in the woods expanded into strangers who loved her, and she went from stage to stage around the country, and when she came back to visit the house at the end of the road she was really surprised by how small it was, how low the ceilings. The gifts she bore, sweaters and jewelry and wallets and watches—knockoffs bought from city sidewalk vendors— seemed to embarrass her family. Her very presence seemed to embarrass them. "You're so thespian," her father murmured in a voice coated with distaste.

"No, I'm not," she said, because she thought he had said "lesbian."

His face had gotten heavier, though he was still lean. He slid a watch across the table to her. "Find someone else who can use this. When have you ever seen me wear a watch?"

But her grandmother, who looked just the same, sat up and said, "You've become beautiful, Annie. How did that happen? Tell me everything." And so Annie sat in the big chair and told her grandmother about dressing rooms and small apartments in different towns and how everyone took care of one another and how she never forgot her lines. Her grandmother said, "Don't come back. Don't get married. Don't have children. All those things will bring you heartache."

*

For a long time Annie did not come back. She sometimes missed her mother, as though she felt across the miles a wave of sadness lapping up to her from Sylvia, but when she telephoned her mother always said "Oh, not much here is new" and did not seem at all interested in what Annie was doing. Her sister never wrote or called, and Jamie very seldom. At Christmastime she sent home boxes of gifts until her mother sighed over the telephone and said, "Your father wants to know what we're to do with all this rubbish." This hurt her feelings, but not lastingly, because those she lived with and knew from the theater were so warm and kind and outraged on her behalf. The older members of any cast treated Annie with tenderness, and so without realizing it she stayed in lots of ways a child. "Your innocence protects you," a director told her once, and in truth she did not know what he meant.

There is a saying that every woman should have three daughters because that way there will be one to take care of you in old age. Annie Appleby was everywhere, California, London, Amsterdam, Pittsburgh, Chicago, and the only place Sylvia could find her was in a gossip magazine at the drugstore, where her name had been linked with that of a famous movie star. This embarrassed Sylvia; people in town learned not to mention it. Cindy was nearby in New

Hampshire; she'd had many children quickly and a husband who wanted her home. So it was Jamie who stayed at the farm, unmarried. Silently he worked alongside his father, who remained strong even with age. Silently Jamie tended to the needs of his grandmother next door. Sylvia often said, "What would I do without you, Jamie?" And he would shake his head. His mother was lonely, he knew. He saw how his father increasingly did not speak with her. His father began to eat sloppily, which he had never done. The sound of his chewing was notable; bits of food fell down onto his shirt. "Elgin, my goodness," Sylvia said, rising to get a napkin, and he shook her off. "For Christ's sake, woman!"

Privately Sylvia said, "What's wrong with your father?" But Jamie shrugged and they did not talk about it again until Jamie, going through the books, realized what was happening. Terribly, it all made sense: his father's querulousness, his sudden asking repeatedly where Annie was, "Where is that child? Is she in the woods again?" All this fell into Jamie's stomach with the silence of a stone falling into the darkness of a well. Within a year they could not care for the man; he ran away, he started a fire in the barn, he drove them insane with his questions, "Where's Annie? Is she in the woods?" And so they found him a home, and Elgin was furious to be there. Sylvia stopped visiting because he was so angry when she came, one time calling her a cow. The sisters were informed, and Cindy came home for a few days, but Annie could not. She said she could be there by spring.

When she turned off Route 4, she was surprised to find that the dirt road had been paved and was no longer a narrow road. A few new and large houses had been added near the Daigle place. She barely recognized where she was. Cindy was in the kitchen, which seemed even smaller than the last time Annie had come home, and when Annie bent to kiss her, Cindy just stood without moving. Their mother, said Jamie, was upstairs; she would be down after the kids had talked. Annie felt the physical, almost electric, aspects of alarm and sank slowly into a chair as she unbuttoned her coat. Jamie spoke carefully and directly. Their father was being asked to leave the home he was in; he was abusive to the orderlies, Jamie said, making sexual passes at all the men, grabbing at their crotches, and was altogether disruptive. A psychiatrist had seen him, and their father had given permission for their talks to be shared, though how a man with dementia could give permission Jamie did not understand, but as a result Sylvia had learned that for years Elgin had had a relationship with Seth Potter, they were lovers, Sylvia said she had often suspected this, and Elgin was, demented as he might be, referring to himself as a raging homosexual, and he was very graphic in things he said; they would most likely have to put him in a far less pleasant place, there was no money unless they sold the farm, and no one was buying potato farms these days.

"All right," Annie finally said. Her siblings had been silent for many minutes, and their faces had seemed so young and sad although they were middle-aged faces with middle-aged lines. "All right, we'll deal with this." She nodded at them reassuringly. Later she went next door to see her grandmother, who seemed surprisingly unchanged. She lay on the couch and watched her granddaughter go about turning on lights. "You came home to deal with your father? Your mother's had a hell of a time."

"Yes," Annie said, and sat in the big chair nearby.

"If you want my opinion, your father went mad because of his behavior. Being a pervert. I always knew he was a homo, and that can drive you insane, and now he's insane, that's my opinion, if you want it."

"I don't," Annie said gently.

"Then tell me something exciting. Where have you been that's exciting?"

Annie looked at her. The old woman's face was as expectant as a child's, and Annie felt an unbidden and almost unbearable gash of compassion for this woman, who had lived in this house for years. She said, "I went to the ambassador's home in London. They had the whole production there for dinner. That was exciting."

"Oh, tell me everything, Annie."

"Let me sit for a minute." And so they were silent, her grandmother lying back down like a young person trying to be patient, and Annie, who up until this very day had always felt like a child—which is why she could not marry, she could not be a wife—now felt quietly ancient. She thought how for years onstage she had used the image of walking up the dirt road holding her father's hand, the snow-covered fields spread around them, the woods in the distance, joy spilling through her—how she had used this scene to have tears immediately come to her eyes, for the happiness of it, and the loss of it. And now she wondered if it had even happened, if the road had ever been narrow and dirt, if her father had ever held her hand and said that his family was the most important thing to him.

"That's right," she had said earlier to her sister, who had cried out that were it true they would have known. What Annie did not say was that there were many ways of not knowing things; her own experience over the years now spread like a piece of knitting in her lap with different colored yarns—some dark—all through it. In her thirties now, Annie had loved men; her heart had often been broken. Currents of treachery and deceit seemed to run everywhere; the forms they took always surprised her. But she had many friends, and they had their disappointments too, and nights and days were spent giving support and being supported; the theater world was a cult, Annie thought. It took care of its own even while it hurt you. She had recently, though, had fantasies of what they called "going normal." Having a house and a husband and children and a garden. The quietness of all that. But what would she do with all the feelings that streamed down her like small rivers? It was not the sound of applause Annie liked—in fact, she often barely heard it—it was the moment onstage when she knew she had left the world and fully joined another. Not unlike the feelings of ecstasy she'd had in the woods as a child.

Her father must have worried she would come across him in the woods. Annie shifted in the big chair.

"Did they tell you about Charlene?" her grandmother said.

"Charlene Daigle?" Annie turned to look at the old woman. "What about her?"

"She's started a chapter for incest people. Incest Survivors, I believe they're called."

"Are you serious?"

"Soon as that father died, she started it. Ran an article in the newspaper, said one out of five children are sexually abused. Honestly, Annie. What a world."

"But that's awful. Poor Charlene!"

"She looked pretty good in her picture. Heavier. She's gotten heavier."

"My God," Annie said softly.

Cindy had said quietly, "We must have been the laughingstock of the county."

"No," Jamie had said to her. "Whatever he did, he hid."

Annie had seen how their distress showed in their guarded faces. "Oh," she had said, feeling maternal, protective, toward them. "It doesn't really matter."

But it did! Oh, it did.

Back in the main house, Sylvia sat with her children for

supper in the kitchen. "I heard about Charlene," Annie said. "It's unbelievably sad."

"If it's true," answered Sylvia.

Annie looked at her siblings, but they looked at the food they moved into their mouths. "Why would it not be true? Why would someone make that up?" Jamie shrugged, and Annie saw—or felt she saw—that Charlene's burdens were nothing to them; their own universe and its wild recent unmooring were all that mattered now. Sylvia went upstairs to bed, and the three siblings sat talking by the wood stove. Jamie especially could not stop talking. Their once silent father in his state of dementia seemed unable to keep himself from spilling forth all he had held on to secretly for years, and Jamie, who had been silent himself, now had to tumble all he heard before them. "One time they saw you in the woods, Annie, and he was always afraid after that that you'd find them." Annie nodded. Cindy looked at her sister with a pained face, as though Annie should have more of a reaction than that. Annie put her hand over her sister's for a moment. "But one of the strangest things he said," Jamie reported, sitting back, "was that he drove us to school so he could, just for those moments, be near Seth Potter. He didn't even see him, dropping us off. But he liked knowing he was close to him each morning. That Seth was only a few feet away, inside the school."

"Oh God, it makes me sick," Cindy said.

Jamie squinted at the wood stove. "It puzzles me, is all."

The vulnerability of their faces Annie could almost not bear. She looked around the small kitchen, the wallpaper with water stains streaking down it, the rocking chair their father had always sat in, the cushion now with a rip large enough to show the stuffing, the teakettle on the stove that had been the same one for years, the curtain across the top of the window with a fine spray of cobwebs between it and the pane. Annie looked back at her siblings. They may not have felt the daily dread that poor Charlene had lived with. But the truth was always there. They had grown up on shame; it was the nutrient of their soil. Yet, oddly, it was her father she felt she understood the best. And for a moment Annie wondered at this, that her brother and sister, good, responsible, decent, fair-minded, had never known the passion that caused a person to risk everything they had, everything they held dear heedlessly put in danger—simply to be near the white dazzle of the sun that somehow for those moments seemed to leave the earth behind.

Gift

Abel Blaine was late.

A meeting with directors from all over the state had gone too long, and all afternoon Abel had sat in the conference room with its rich cherry table stretching like a dark ice rink down the center, the people around it trying to sit up straighter the more tired they became. A young girl from the Rockford region, who Abel felt was carefully dressed for her first company presentation—he was moved by this—had talked on and on, people looking at Abel with increasing panic—*Make her stop*—because he was the man in charge. Perspiring lightly, he had finally stood and put his papers into his briefcase, and thanked the girl—woman, woman! you could not call them girls these days, for the love of God—and she blushed and sat down and didn't seem to know where to look for a few minutes until people on their way out spoke to her nicely, as did Abel himself.

Then Abel was finally in his car, on the expressway, then steering through the narrow snowy streets, and pleased, as he so often was, by the sight of his large brick house, which tonight had a tiny white light twinkling from each window.

His wife opened the door and said, "Oh, Abel, you forgot." Above the collar of her red dress, little green Christmas ball earrings moved.

He said, "I got here as fast as I could, Elaine."

"He forgot," she said to Zoe, and Zoe said, "Well, you can't eat, Dad, we had to feed the kids and we're really late."

"I won't eat," Abel said.

Zoe's tightened mouth caused a brief cramping of his bowels, but the grandchildren were clapping their hands and yelling "Grandpa, Grandpa!" and his wife was telling him to hurry, *please* would he hurry, dear *God*. Abel had entered a period in life in which he acknowledged that the Christmas season tended to make people irritable, yet his own sense of Christmas—lit trees and happy children and stockings that sagged from the mantel—he could not seem to give up.

Walking through the lobby of the Littleton Theater, he saw that he did not have to give anything up, for here it was: the town together as it was each year, little girls in plaid shiny dresses, boys wide-eyed and wearing shirts with collars as though they were miniature men; there was the priest from the Episcopal church—soon to retire and be replaced by a lesbian, which Abel gamely accepted, though he'd have liked Father Harcroft to stay on forever; there was the head of the school board; and there was Eleanor Shawtuck, who had been at the meeting today, now giving Abel a wave with a widening of her smile; they were all getting settled into their seats, murmurs and shushes, the final diminution of sound. A whisper: "Grandpa, my dress is getting squished." His sweet Sophia, who held her plastic pony with its pink hair tightly in her fist; he moved his already cramped leg and let her shake out her skirt, whispering to her that she was the prettiest girl there, and she said, a little too loudly, "Snowball has never seen a play before," bouncing the pony on her knee. The lights dimmed, the show began.

Abel closed his eyes and was immediately visited by the vision of his sister, Dottie, two hours away in Jennisberg, outside of Peoria, and what would she be doing on Christmas Day? His concern—his love—for her was genuine, yet the responsibility he felt toward her revolted him in a way he'd admit to no one. It was because she was alone and unhappy, he thought, his eyes opening. But she might not be unhappy, and she might not be alone either, since she ran a bed-and-breakfast and could keep it open, he supposed, for the holiday. He would telephone her from work tomorrow. His wife could not abide her.

He squeezed Sophia's hand and gave his attention to the show, which was as familiar to him as a church service. How many years had they been coming to see *A Christmas Carol*? First with Zoe and her brothers, and now with Zoe's own children, sweet Sophia and her older brother, Jake.

Confusedly, Abel's mind could not quite connect itself either to his sister's life or to the youth of his children; inside him was a tiny gasp at the ungraspable concept of time going by. From onstage came the hearty and false-sounding "A merry Christmas, Uncle!" Then the slamming of a thin door that seemed as if it might topple. "Bah, humbug!" came Scrooge's reply.

Hunger descended with a rush. Abel pictured pork chops and almost groaned; fantastical images came to him of roasted potatoes and boiled onions. He crossed his legs, uncrossed them, bumping his knee into the woman who sat in front of him, and he leaned forward to whisper, "Sorry, sorry!" He felt that she grimaced slightly; he'd overdone it with the apology. In the dim light he shook his head once.

The show seemed ponderously slow.

He glanced at Sophia, who was staring at the stage attentively. He glanced at Zoe, who cast her eyes over him with a coldness he did not understand. Onstage, Scrooge was scrambling about his bedroom as Marley's Ghost appeared in chains. "You are fettered," said Scrooge to the ghost. "Tell me why."

A thought came to Abel like a bat that swooped from the eaves: Zoe was unhappy. The thought became a dark shape in his lap, as though he was required to hold it there.

But no.

Zoe had little kids who kept her very busy, and this was not unhappiness.

Her husband had stayed in Chicago tonight because he had to work, as a lawyer about to be made partner must do. There was nothing wrong with Zoe. She belonged to the privileged layer of society, to what was referred to these days as the *one percent,* and this was due partly to the hard work and perseverance of her father. Decency was why he was where he was. People had always known to trust him, and trust in business was everything. Zoe had chosen to marry a man who would keep her in this position, and there was nothing wrong with that, *not one thing.* He had argued with his son-in-law only once, when the young man suggested ways for Abel to not pay so much in taxes. "I only thought—" the fellow began.

"That I am a Republican and don't believe in big government—and you are right—but I will pay my taxes." Recalling this, he never understood the fury he had felt.

Abel now took a deep, unquiet breath and sat up straight; he discreetly checked his pulse and found it to be high.

Onstage, Scrooge was peering through the filthy night-time window. Then he was on his bed listening to the ding-dongs of the bell, then he was off his bed, agitated, saying, "It can't be!" Abel recalled—at that moment—how his wife had handed him the newspaper at breakfast a few days earlier, tapping with her finger one column. Linck McKenzie, the man who played Scrooge, might be a favorite with the townspeople, he might be a favorite with the students he taught in the MFA program at Littleton College, but he was no favorite of the critic who wrote that he was a lucky man, this Mr. Linck McKenzie, being the only person in the theater who did not have to watch his own performance.

Elaine and Abel had agreed: The review was gratuitously mean. And then Abel had forgotten it. But now the words affected him. Now it seemed that Scrooge really was ridiculous, that the entire thing was arguably ridiculous. It seemed to Abel that everyone was loudly *reciting a line,* and this caused him discomfort, as though he'd not be able to leave the theater without thinking that everyone he met was reciting a line. Surely going to the theater should not have that effect on a person. He glanced down at sweet Sophia, and she gave him the compressed, fleeting smile of a polite young woman. He squeezed her knee and she became a little girl again, ducking her head, then holding his hand, with the plastic pony gripped in her other.

The Ghost of Christmas Past was saying, "A solitary child, neglected by his friends, is left there still." And Scrooge began to cry. The sound was phony, dismissible. Abel closed his eyes. Sophia's hand slipped from his; he folded his hands on his lap, and soon he was falling asleep. He knew this because of the incongruity of his thoughts, and felt gratitude that he could give himself over to the pleasant exhaustion rolling up against his shoulders; he remembered, and it was like a yellow light shining in the dusk behind his closed eyes, how he had seen Lucy Barton last year when she came to Chicago on her book tour, Lucy Barton, the daughter of his mother's cousin, oh, that poor girl, and yet there she was, an older woman, and he had stepped into the bookstore and waited in line to have his book signed, and she had said, *Abel,* and risen, and tears had come into her eyes—all this made him feel happy as he felt himself falling into sleep, but then he was trying to find his mother, riding in an elevator that would not stop when the buttons were pushed, then he was in a narrow hallway, searching for her, going one way then another, sensing her in the darkness—and she was gone; even deep inside the dream he recognized the ancient, unquenchable longing that was not quite panic— He woke as gasps came from the audience.

The lights had gone out. The stage was in darkness. The actors had stopped speaking. Only the EXIT signs shone above the doors. And the rows of lights like bright buttons on the floor of the aisle. Abel could feel fear rising around him like dark water. Sophia began to cry, and other children were crying too. "Mommy?" Abel scooped up the tiny Sophia and tucked her onto his lap. "Ssh," he said, spreading his hand across the back of her warm head. "It's nothing, it will be fine." Still, the child cried. Zoe's voice said, "Honey, I'm right here."

How long it stayed dark Abel could not have said, probably no more than a few minutes, but what he was most aware of during this strange time was the number of families that began to argue strenuously, his own included. Elaine said, "Abel, get us out of here. Watch the children." Already in the darkness people were trying to scramble to the aisle, some flipping on cellphones for the light, so that wrists and cuffs were illuminated in what seemed to be disembodied flickers of an ectoplasmic presence. Zoe said, "Mom, stop. This is how people get trampled to death. Dad, hold Sophia, I've got Jake."

"I want us *out* of here, Abel," his wife said. "And if you—"

After many years of marriage things get said, scenes occur, and there is a cumulative effect as well. All this sped through Abel's heart, that the tenderness between husband and wife had long been attenuating and that he might have to live the rest of his life without it. A sound came from him.

"Dad? Are you okay?" The light of Zoe's cellphone was aimed toward him.

"I'm fine, honey," he said. "We'll wait. Just as you say."

A voice from the stage called out for folks to remain calm, and then the lights came on, catching families in their various states of panic and disarray. The Blaine family remained where they were—not every family did—and they watched as the show at last continued, but the tension of the event could not fully dissipate, and when, finally, the lights went out, the applause was that of relief.

They were silent in the car, and only when they were close to home did Abel glance in the rearview mirror to ask Sophia if she had been able to enjoy the show in spite of the mishap. "What's mishap?" she asked.

Zoe said, "When something goes wrong. Like tonight when the lights went out."

"But *why* did the lights go out?" Jake asked quietly.

"We don't know," Abel said. "Sometimes a fuse gets blown. No harm done."

"Exit signs are lit by generators." This was Elaine's contribution. "Thank God emergency lights are required by law to have separate sources of energy."

"Mom, let's just leave this alone," said Zoe tiredly. Perhaps Zoe, as grown children so frequently did, found fault with her parents' marriage, had glimpsed the waning of tenderness over the years, felt for them a deep aversion: *My marriage will never be like yours, Dad.* Fine, he would have said, that's fine, honey.

Hungry as he was, he sat with his grandchildren after they were in their pajamas. He made them laugh doing imitations of Scrooge, wanting to rid them of any fear. Sophia suddenly slid from his knee, and in a moment she screamed. It was a piercing, horrifying sound, and she ran into the bedroom where the grandchildren always stayed; the screaming turned to sobs.

Snowball was nowhere to be found.

The car was searched quickly and thoroughly. No plastic pony with bright pink hair was discovered. "I think she left it in the theater, Dad." Zoe looked at him with apology, and Abel got the car keys and said to Sophia, "I will return with your pony."

He was dizzy with fatigue.

"Another mizzap," said Sophia, bashfully. "Right, Grandpa?"

"You go to sleep." He bent to kiss her. "And when you wake up in the morning, all will be well."

※

Driving through the darkened streets, crossing over the river into the center of town, he worried that the theater would be closed. He parked his car on the street and found that the front door of the theater did not yield, nor could anyone be seen through the dark glass. He fumbled for his cellphone and discovered that in his hurry he had left the phone behind. Very quietly he swore, then ran his hand over his mouth. A young man appeared, coming out a side door. Abel called out "Wait!" The fellow must be a theater student, Abel surmised, because he smiled at Abel, and held the door, and when Abel said, "My granddaughter left her toy pony here," the fellow said, "I think the stage manager is still around, maybe he can help you."

So Abel was inside. But it was dark and he did not know exactly where he was, as the door he had entered was a side door and seemingly led backstage. Tentatively he touched the wall for a light switch and found none as he stepped forward slowly. But then—ha! He flipped it, but saw only a dim light respond from the distance, enough to illuminate the narrow hallway before him. Yellow-painted brick walls marked with graffiti were on each side of him. He knocked on the first door he saw, and found it to be locked. "Hello?" He called the word out cheerfully, but there was no answer. The place smelled familiar and unmistakably theatrical.

His hunger caused the hallway to seem very long. Abel saw, between two black curtains, what must be the stage. Above him were dark rows of stage lights, unlit, like enormous beetles, waiting. "Hello," he called again, and again there was no answer, though he sensed now the presence of someone. "Hello? I'm trying to find the stage manager, hello? My granddaughter left her—"

Turning right, he saw above him the pony hanging from a small noose of clothesline that was looped over a bare unlit bulb in the hallway. Snowball, her plastic feet pointing in front of her, her pink hair sticking out from her head, was caught in a look of eternal dismay; her eyes were wide open, their long dark lashes coquettishly splayed.

Behind him was the sudden sound of a door opening, and he turned. There was Linck McKenzie, Scrooge, with his wig off but his makeup still on, which made him look half-crazed. "Hello," said Abel, holding forth his hand. "My granddaughter left her pony here—" He nodded at it hanging from the lightbulb. "I imagine some student was having a bit of fun, but I need to bring it home or I'll lose the child's respect, I'm afraid."

Scrooge returned the handshake. His hand was bony and strong and very dry. "Come in," Scrooge said, as though it were an office he was occupying, but it was, Abel saw as he entered, a small square room that must have been used for storage; it had dropcloths and old lamps and a table missing a leg.

Abel said, "I'm afraid I need a stepladder or a chair. Oh, there—" In the corner was an old-fashioned-looking chair with a curved armrest.

Scrooge shut the door behind him and said, "Well, there's only that one chair, so why don't you sit."

"Oh no, no, I hardly need to—"

Scrooge jerked his head in the direction of the chair. "I want you to sit."

Abel understood then that he was in the presence of instability, but oddly this only caused an increase in his enervation, and after a moment he said politely, "I think I'll stand, thank you. Is there something I can help you with?" He smiled benignly at Scrooge, who remained leaning against the door. Abel wanted to say, How long do you think this will take? Realizing this was his thought, he understood that he was removed from himself in a way distinct and strange.

Scrooge said, "I'd like to *say* some things, you see. Then when I'm done, you can go. You'll manage. You strike me as the kind of old man who thinks he's in good shape because so far you've not had a heart attack." A mirthless smile came to Scrooge as he studied Abel. "Your clothes are expensive." He nodded. "A devoted secretary organizes your days. Nothing is *really* expected of you anymore, you're a figurehead. A few leadership qualities left. But physical strength, I doubt you have much. So please. Sit."

Abel stayed exactly where he was, but he felt winded. Everything this wretched man had said was essentially— except for the part about not having had a heart attack yet—true. The heart attack had been only a year ago and had scared Abel severely. He took two steps toward the chair and sat down; the chair swiveled backward, surprising him.

"Weak in the knees," Scrooge said. "Well, I'm strong as wire. I'm also at the end of my rope. No one should be in a room with a man who's at the end of his rope." He laughed, showing his fillings, and Abel now felt a true bolt of alarm. He wondered how long he would have to be gone before his wife—or perhaps Zoe—would drive to the theater, God in heaven.

"That pony belongs to your grandchild?"

"It does," Abel said. "She's very attached to it."

"I hate children," Scrooge said. He slid down the wall and sat on the floor cross-legged. He was not a young man; Abel was surprised at his suppleness. "They're little, they move quickly, they're *very* judgmental. You look surprised."

"This whole thing is surprising." Abel tried to smile, but Scrooge did not smile. Abel continued, his mouth dry, "Look, I'm awfully sorry, but can we—"

"Why are you sorry?"

"Well, I suppose—"

"You're stuck in a room with a lunatic and you apologize?"

"I see what you mean. Well, I would like to go, if you think—"

"I *think* I would like to say a few things. I told you that. The first thing I'd like to say is that I'm deeply, deeply tired of the theater. I only went into it because it takes everyone, especially if you were born queer back when I was, it scoops you up and gives you a sense of belonging—which is false, phony, silliness. And the second thing I would like to say is that I caused the lights to go out tonight. I did it with a cellphone inside my nightshirt. It's all on the Internet, you know, pretty soon you'll be able to blow up a whole country with a cellphone. But I followed the directions and I was quite surprised. I wanted to cause chaos and I did. Anyway, I had no one to tell. I was quite pleased with myself, and now find it to be a hollow victory."

"Are you serious?"

"About the hollow victory?"

"About the lights."

"Completely. Awesome, as the kids would say." Scrooge shook his head slowly. Accentuating his words with a pointed index finger aimed at Abel, he said, "We *all* want an audience. If we do something, and no one knows we did it?— Well, then the tree might not have fallen in the forest." His face opened in surprise. "So there. Now I've reported it, it happened, I'm satisfied. Though not as satisfied as I expected to be, honestly. And what are we going to do with you? You'll walk out of here and tell the police, or your wife, and eventually Linck McKenzie will be even more of a joke. The town can watch him go down."

"I'm not interested in that," Abel said.

"You might be tomorrow. Or the day after."

"I'm interested in getting the pony back to my grand-daughter."

After a long pause, Scrooge said, "It's the oddest thing. But that just makes me *hurt* with jealousy. You probably want to say, 'If you had a grandchild yourself, Mr. Oddball Theater Queer, you might understand that love.'"

"I wasn't thinking that at all. That's not close to any-thing I was thinking. I was thinking about Sophia. Waiting for her pony. I hope she's been able to fall asleep."

Scrooge frowned. "Sophia. I suppose this little girl is well off?"

Abel waited a moment before he said, "She is, yes."

"When you were her age, were you rich?"

"I was not remotely rich."

"And did you get rich by working hard?"

Abel again hesitated. "I work hard," he said. "I have al-ways worked hard."

Scrooge clapped his hands. "Ha! I bet you *married* your wealth! Don't blush, old man. It's terribly American, it's fine. Nothing to be ashamed of. Oh, I've really embarrassed you. Quick, quick, let's change the subject. This Sophia—do you think she'll be a hard worker too? I'm concerned. I don't think people work hard anymore. And these kids—

I heard that some preschooler got a gold star just for show-ing up for the week! My dear man, you've turned red as a beet."

Scrooge looked around the room and saw what he ap-parently wanted, a plastic bottle of water; he scuttled over to it, and returned, handing it to Abel. Abel did not argue. He had become desperately warm beneath his woolen suit. He drank, then offered the bottle to Scrooge, who shook his head, sitting once more with his back to the wall.

"What business are you in?" Scrooge asked. A toothpick was lying on the table, and he took it and picked at his teeth.

"Air-conditioning units." Abel fleetingly pictured the young girl in the conference room today, so overprepared for her presentation; she was from Rockford, where he had grown up. "People still work hard," he said.

"Air conditioning. You make a bundle."

"And every year I give to the arts."

Scrooge tilted his head, looking at Abel. His lips were colorless, cracked in places. "Now, please," he said quietly. "Don't be like that."

Abel said nothing. A private nail of shame was driven into his chest; he could feel himself perspire. He remem-bered how earlier he'd thought of people reciting a line, and he understood now that he was one of them.

"Look," Scrooge continued. "I just need you to listen to me and then you can go."

Abel shook his head. A disc of nausea spun through him, he felt saliva rushing to his mouth. In his mind arrived a full understanding: Zoe *was* unhappy.

"I've scared you," Scrooge said, in a voice that seemed to have scared Scrooge as well.

Abel said quietly, "My daughter's unhappy."

Scrooge asked, "How old is she?"

"Thirty-five. Married to a very successful lawyer. Has wonderful kids."

Scrooge blew out his breath slowly. "Well, sounds like death to me."

"Why?" Abel asked sincerely. "It should be perfect."

"Perfectly lonely. A successful lawyer's never around. She loves her kids, but it bores her, all the kid chores. And she feels irritated with the nanny and the cleaning woman, and her husband doesn't want to hear it—and so she doesn't like going to bed with him anymore, that's a chore now too. And she looks at the rest of her life and thinks, God, what is this? Her kids will grow up, and then she's really in Dullsville, and she'll buy a new bracelet, and then a new pair of shoes, and maybe that will help for five minutes, but she gets more and more anxious and pretty soon they'll put her on Valium or antidepressants, because society's been drugging its women for years—"

Abel held up a hand to indicate that he should stop.

Scrooge said, "I know you want to go. You will, you will. Relax." Scrooge opened his mouth wide, poked at something with the toothpick, then expelled the bit with a large sigh. "Sorry," he said. "That was gross."

Almost imperceptibly Abel nodded, to indicate that it was okay with him.

Earlier in the month Abel had celebrated a birthday that put him smack in the middle of his sixties. You look great, people said. You look wonderful. No one said: Your capped teeth—your pride and joy so long ago—seem to get bigger as you get older. No one said: Abel, too bad about those teeth. And maybe no one thought it.

"So *dumb*," Scrooge said. "The telling-someone-to-relax thing. When did you ever relax because someone told you to?"

"I don't know," Abel said.

"Probably never." The tone of Scrooge's voice had become gentle, conversational, as though he'd known Abel a long time.

Had he more energy, Abel might then have told this strange and tortured man how, many years ago, he had worked as an usher at the theater in Rockford, just steps away from the Rock River, and that's what he had smelled tonight when he'd entered the side door, that secret scent of theater. He had secured the job during high school. Sixteen years old. The very year that his little sister had been brought before her sixth-grade class, the stain on her dress pointed to, and told that no one was ever too poor to buy sanitary pads. Dottie had not wanted to return to school after that, and Abel had promised her something, he could not remember what. What he did remember was the power of those paychecks. At sixteen he had learned the astonishing power of money. The only thing money could not buy was a friend for Dottie (or for him, but that did not matter as much), but it bought a twinkling bracelet, that's what she got! And that had made her smile. Most of all, money bought food.

And this made him think of Lucy Barton again, how terribly poor she had been as well, how when he went as a kid to stay with her family a few weeks each summer she would go with him to look for food in the dumpster behind Chatwin's Cake Shoppe. (Oh, the look on Lucy's face when she saw him last year in that bookstore, all that time having passed by! She held his hand with both of hers, and did not want to let it go.)

What puzzled Abel about life was how much one forgot but then lived with anyway—like phantom limbs, he supposed. Because he could not honestly say anymore what he'd felt when he'd found food in a dumpster. Gladness, perhaps, when he discovered large parts of a steak that could be scraped clean. It gets terribly practical, he told his wife many years later. Then came the moment of her ill-concealed horror: *Weren't you ashamed?* And the answer— the understanding—so immediate that it was coming to him even as she spoke: Well, then you've never been hungry, Elaine. He did not say it. But he did become ashamed, once his wife asked him that question. Then he surely became ashamed. She requested that he never tell their children how their father had been so poor as to eat from garbage cans.

"It has made me sick," Scrooge said. "I believe it's made me ill. I've been teaching these little devil-brats for twenty-eight years."

"You don't enjoy it?" Abel was aware of a sense of cognitive distance, and he hoped he had asked the right question.

"Oh, it's the most perverse thing in the world." Scrooge waved a hand in annoyance. "We take the students with money, you know. Unless there's no rich crier. We always need a crier, of course, someone who can cry on demand. Criers always think they're particularly sensitive, particularly talented, but criers are just particularly nuts, is what they are." Scrooge appeared exhausted, and rested his head against the wall, looking up at the ceiling.

"Say, what I think—" Abel started, but it took him a moment to find the words. "I think you're upset about that review—"

"*Hey.*" Scrooge was suddenly on his feet. He pointed a finger at Abel. "Don't you even. Trust me on this, Mr. Fancy Pants. I've been coming to the end of my rope for a very long time." He pulled a cigarette from his shirt pocket. He didn't light it, just tapped it against his leg. "I told you at the start I felt like talking. And we were doing that. Talking. Okay? I want to *talk*. We were *talking*."

Abel nodded. "We were."

"So then," Scrooge said, exhaling a big sigh and sliding his back down the wall slowly until he was seated on the floor again. "Where were we? You were getting ready to marry your way to the top."

"For the love of God." Abel forced himself to sit up straighter. "We are not going to discuss my wife." He spoke in almost a whisper. His mind did not know where to put itself. Fatigue was like a piece of cloth covering him.

"Okay. We won't discuss her." Scrooge was quiet for a moment, and then— "But I've been lonely," he said.

Abel looked at this man, whose face was looking up at him now, the scalp still with its gray streaks from where the wig had been. "I understand," Abel said.

"You understand?" Scrooge asked.

Abel almost smiled, but he did not know why he had the impulse to smile. And then surprisingly—horribly!—he felt he would weep. Only barely did he prevent himself, but it affected his speech. "Because—I am too." Scrooge nodded with what seemed to Abel to be a simplicity of understanding, and Abel said, "Say, I could be your crier."

Scrooge said, "Not nutty enough. But you're honest. Oh, thank the *gods*. I wanted to talk to a person, and here you are a real person, you have no idea how hard it is—to find a real person."

They were both silent for a moment, as though such a

thing needed to be absorbed. Then Scrooge said, "Did you like your mother?" His voice—to Abel's ears—was almost childlike again.

"I liked her." Abel heard himself saying this. "I loved her."

"No daddy around?"

It was strange for Abel to hear this phrase, reminiscent of a schoolyard taunt, yet it was not a taunt now. Still, he felt flushed. No, his daddy had died when Abel was very young. Once, briefly—was it days only?—there had been a man, and Abel remembered it mostly because after the man left, Dottie had got a store-bought dress and Abel had been bought a new pair of pants. These pants became too short quickly, and stayed that way almost a year. But they were the pants that allowed him the job as an usher, after his mother's cousin—Lucy Barton's mother—who did sewing had managed to lengthen them when he'd gone to stay with them.

"Oh, I can see the question hurt your feelings," Scrooge said. "I can be awfully insensitive. And then I get pissed off at people because I myself am sensitive. I don't like sensitive people who only feel sensitive for themselves."

"I'm sorry," Abel said, blinking his eyes, which seemed blurry. "You know—I'm not feeling very well. You see, I had a heart attack a year ago."

Scrooge was on his feet again. "Why didn't you *tell* me? Jesus. Let's get you help."

"No worries," Abel said. "Do you think you could get the pony down for my granddaughter?"

Scrooge looked at him so searchingly that Abel looked away; he had not been looked at that closely—that intimately—in years. "'No worries'?" the man said in a voice almost tender. "Who *are* you?"

"A man who dresses well," Abel answered, once more aware of the bizarre impulse to smile. "A man who doesn't cheat on his taxes." And again—the bizarre impulse to almost weep.

"You *do* dress well." Scrooge opened the door and was gone from Abel's sight. Abel heard him calling, "I've always known a tailor-made suit! Now I'm getting that pony and don't you move. Stay calm, and stay right there!"

Abel's tailor had been a man from London named Keith, and twice a year Abel strode into the Drake Hotel, arriving at a suite that provided vast views of the lake. In these overheated rooms, while the radiators hissed, Abel would be measured by Keith with a cloth tape, and in gestures so subtle, so assured and quick, Keith would place muslin against Abel's shoulders, his chest, down the length of his arm, marking it with chalk. The swatches of fabric were laid out in the other room, and almost always Abel chose what Keith suggested. Only once or twice did Abel suggest that perhaps the fabric be more subdued, or that the stripes might just be—perhaps—too wide. "I don't want to look like a gangster," Abel joked, and Keith answered, "Oh, surely not."

When word came that Keith had died of cancer, Abel was astonished. That astonishment had to do with death, with the wiping out of a person, with the puzzlement that the man was simply gone. The simplicity of the goneness was something Abel was familiar with; he was not a young man, he had known the death of others, starting with the goneness of his own father. But what followed this astonishment was a searing sense of shame, as though Abel had done something unsavory all those years by having Keith build his clothes. He found himself murmuring the words out loud, when he was in his car, or alone in his office, or getting dressed in the morning, "I'm sorry. God, I'm so sorry."

Even while he voted as a conservative, even while he took his annual bonus from the board, even while he ate in the best restaurants Chicago offered, and even while most of him thought what he had thought for years, I will not apologize for being rich, he did apologize, but to whom precisely he did not know. Waves of shame would suddenly pour over him, the way his wife had endured hot flashes for years, her face instantly bright red, rivulets of perspiration forming on the sides of her face. She could not be jovial about these incidents, the way he saw some women at the office were. But he felt he understood better now, the uncontrolled assault she must have felt, just as he felt the uncontrolled assault of his shame, which, he was perfectly aware, had no basis in anything real. Keith had had a job. He had done his job well. He had been paid well. (He had not really been paid that well.)

But when Abel came across two men in the manufacturing department one day, the first making a snide remark about "being part of a company involved with sheer corporate greed," the second rolling his eyes, replying, "Don't be a stupid, cynical youth," it was this second man that infuriated Abel, who said to him, "We *need* the cynicism of youth, it's healthy. Stop degrading the efforts of mankind by calling them stupid, for the love of God!" He worried about this later, because the workplace was not what it had been for most of his career, it was now a petri dish of potential lawsuits, and Human Resources was kept busy, though admittedly far less than at other companies. Abel was, in fact, respected. He was even loved. (Dearly, by his longtime secretary.)

But the point was—the sense of apology did not go away; it was a tiring thing to carry.

"I married way up," Abel said out loud, and for some reason he wanted to chuckle. "Oh, I did. She seemed as lovely as a Christmas tree to me. I don't mean she looked like a tree, just that she represented all—"

"Here we go, here we go." Linck McKenzie was back, holding out his hand.

"Thank you," Abel said. He saw Linck McKenzie standing in the doorway; he heard Linck say, "You know, you're a good man."

But a darkening came now to the edges of Abel's vision, and a sudden pain moved through his chest; in a moment he thought he might be sliding from his chair. He heard Linck on a telephone, saying *Hurry,* and this made him remember something earlier, Please, would you hurry, but he could not place it, and then there were lots of sounds and doors opening, and he saw an orange strip that he understood he would be placed upon.

A woman large and muscular enough that he thought she was a man, her hair cut short like a man's, was in a uniform and helping—"dyke" is what she'd once have been called, this went through Abel's mind. What marvelous authority she had as she got him on that strip of orange stretcher, asked him if he knew his name. He must have said it, because she began to talk to him. "You stay right with me, Mr. Blaine."

"I'm sorry," Linck kept saying in his ear. Or maybe Abel was the one saying it. He wanted to say "taxes." He did not know if he said it, but he wanted to say to this marvelous woman, strong as a man, that she was what the taxes were for.

"Mr. Blaine, I have your granddaughter's pony with me. Do you know the name of your granddaughter's pony?" this big square woman asked.

He must have said it right because she said, "You hold

right on to Snowball, we're going to take you to the hospital. Are you able to understand me?" He felt a hard plastic thing placed in his hand.

Linck's face was there as they closed the door of the ambulance; he seemed to be saying something.

Abel shook his head. He thought he shook his head, he could not tell, but he wanted to tell Linck McKenzie—so ludicrous that it was absolutely liberating—that he'd had a lovely time, which must be ridiculous but was not. He felt the chill of a fluid filling his veins, and so perhaps they had hooked him up to something and given him a drug, he couldn't find the words to ask— And then later, as the ambulance went faster, Abel felt not fear but a strange exquisite joy, the bliss of things finally and irretrievably out of his control, unpeeled, unpeeling now. Yet there was a streak of something else, as though just outside his reach was the twinkle of a light, as though a Christmas window was there; this puzzled him and pleased him, and in his state of tired ecstasy it seemed almost to come to him. Linck McKenzie's voice: "You're a good man." This made Abel smile even as his chest felt as if rocks were piled upon it. The calm voice of that wonderful big woman told him, "Mr. Blaine, you hold right on," and he thought perhaps his smile appeared to them as a grimace of pain, but what did it matter, he was moving very quickly and easily away now, leaving them, flying—how fast he was going!—past fields of green soybeans, with the most exquisite understanding: He had a friend. He would have said this if he could, he would have said it, but there was no need: Like his sweet Sophia who loved her Snowball, Abel had a friend. And if such a gift could come to him at such a time, then anything—dear girl from Rockford dressed up for her meeting, rushing above the Rock River—he opened his eyes, and yes, there it was, the perfect knowledge: Anything was possible for anyone.

ACKNOWLEDGMENTS

The author wishes to thank the following people for their help with this book:

Jim Tierney, Kathy Chamberlain, Susan Kamil, Beverly Gologorsky, Molly Friedrich, Lucy Carson, Frank Connors (a wonderful storyteller in his own right), and the inimitable Benjamin Dreyer.

ABOUT THE AUTHOR

ELIZABETH STROUT is the Pulitzer Prize–winning author of *Olive Kitteridge;* the #1 *New York Times* bestseller *My Name Is Lucy Barton; The Burgess Boys,* a *New York Times* bestseller; *Abide with Me,* a national bestseller and Book Sense pick; and *Amy and Isabelle,* which won the *Los Angeles Times* Art Seidenbaum Award for First Fiction and the *Chicago Tribune* Heartland Prize. She has also been a finalist for the PEN/Faulkner Award and the Orange Prize in England. Her short stories have been published in a number of magazines, including *The New Yorker* and *O: The Oprah Magazine.* Elizabeth Strout lives in New York City.

elizabethstrout.com
Facebook.com/elizabethstroutfans
Twitter: @LizStrout

To inquire about booking Elizabeth Strout
for a speaking engagement, please contact the
Penguin Random House Speakers Bureau at
speakers@penguinrandomhouse.com.

ABOUT THE TYPE

This book was set in Sabon, a typeface designed by the well-known German typographer Jan Tschichold (1902–74). Sabon's design is based upon the original letter forms of sixteenth-century French type designer Claude Garamond and was created specifically to be used for three sources: foundry type for hand composition, Linotype, and Monotype. Tschichold named his typeface for the famous Frankfurt typefounder Jacques Sabon (c. 1520–80).